"I'm pregnant."

"Oh. Congratulations." In that moment he didn't know what else to say. He wondered why she was telling him now.

Melissa hung her head and let out a sigh, looking incredibly guilty about something. It occurred to him that she might have been in a relationship when they got together and was now remorseful, or worried he'd tell someone.

"If you're with someone, it's okay. I won't say anything about us."

She took a gulp of tea before she spoke. "I'm not with anyone, Lachlan. I haven't been with another man since the festival. In fact, you're the only man I've slept with in eighteen months."

It took a moment for him to process what she was saying, the enormity of those few words eventually flooring him. There was so much wrapped up in that night they'd spent together, it was always going to be more than a casual thing. Although he didn't know the details of Melissa's personal life, they'd clearly both been going through an emotional time.

"So..." He wanted her to spell it out for him.

"You're the father of my baby."

Dear Reader,

Anyone who has ever been under the care of a midwife will know what an amazing job they do. Not only do they go through extensive training, but they often go above and beyond to help reassure expectant mothers. My own midwife was there when I was pregnant with both of my sons, during some difficult times. I'm also lucky enough to have a friend who works in this incredible field, and I hope I've done a good job honoring them both in this book!

Melissa is my strong, capable midwife. But like all expectant parents, she's worried about the future. Especially as it's an unplanned pregnancy. Things get complicated still when her one-night stand walks back into her life determined to be a good father to their baby.

Naturally, their road to parenthood isn't a smooth one, and I hope you enjoy going on this emotional journey with Melissa and Lachlan.

Happy reading!

Karin xx

MIDWIFE'S ONE-NIGHT BABY SURPRISE

KARIN BAINE

MEDICAL ROMANCE

 **Harlequin**®
MEDICAL
ROMANCE

Recycling programs for this product may not exist in your area.

ISBN-13: 978-1-335-59556-0

Midwife's One-Night Baby Surprise

Copyright © 2024 by Karin Baine

 Harlequin Enterprises ULC
22 Adelaide St. West, 41st Floor
Toronto, Ontario M5H 4E3, Canada
www.Harlequin.com

Printed in U.S.A.

Karin Baine lives in Northern Ireland with her husband, two sons and her out-of-control notebook collection. Her mother and her grandmother's vast collection of books inspired her love of reading and her dream of becoming a Harlequin author. Now she can tell people she has a *proper* job! You can follow Karin on Twitter @karinbaine1 or visit her website for the latest news, karinbaine.com.

Books by Karin Baine

Harlequin Medical Romance

Carey Cove Midwives

Festive Fling to Forever

Royal Docs

Surgeon Prince's Fake Fiancée
A Mother for His Little Princess

A GP to Steal His Heart
Single Dad for the Heart Doctor
Falling Again for the Surgeon
Nurse's Risk with the Rebel
An American Doctor in Ireland

Harlequin Romance

Pregnant Princess at the Altar
Highland Fling with Her Boss

Visit the Author Profile page
at Harlequin.com for more titles.

With thanks to Catherine and Karen for sharing
their midwifery knowledge with me.

I may have used some artistic license,
and any mistakes are entirely my own!

**Praise for
Karin Baine**

CHAPTER ONE

'I *AM* ENJOYING MYSELF. Honestly.'

Melissa Moran adjusted her sparkly pink cowboy hat, careful not to smudge the glittery make-up dabbed at her temples, and forced a smile.

Lydia, who was more like family than a friend, wasn't fooled, heaving out a sigh of disappointment. 'Mel...this was all for you.'

Melissa's smile faltered. 'I know, and I appreciate everything you've done. Thank you.'

Lydia folded her arms, straining the leopard print fabric of her jumpsuit across her ample bust. 'Look, I know you've had a rough eighteen months, but this is your thirtieth birthday. Not your hundredth. You're still young. You have a life to live.'

'Unlike Chris,' Melissa mumbled.

'It was an awful, tragic thing, losing him like that when you had all those plans together. But he's gone, Mel. You're still here, and he would want you to have fun.' Lydia grabbed her by the shoulders and gave her a shake.

No, he would want her to be Mrs O'Kane, with a baby on her hip, the way they'd planned. As would she. But fate had cruelly stolen that dream from both of them. Instead of a quiet family birthday celebration, she'd been whisked over to the remote Scottish isle of Innis Holm for a music festival she had no interest in attending. She was trying to enjoy herself for her friend's sake, but it just wasn't her scene. Slopping through the mud, sleeping in a tent, and the prospect of having to use those so-called communal toilets, was not her idea of a good time. Still, Melissa didn't have anyone else, and hadn't had since she was eighteen and her parents had moved abroad.

On the verge of doing her exams, and unwilling to leave everything familiar to her, she'd stayed in Scotland. Though choosing her own path hadn't made her feel any less abandoned or lonely. She'd had to work menial jobs to support her studies until she'd qualified as a midwife. Meeting Chris, finding someone who wanted to settle down as much as she did, had seemed like the perfect fairy tale ending.

Their five-year plan, building up a nest egg so they could get married, was just coming to fruition when he complained of an agonising headache and neck pain. Symptoms she didn't realise at the time were from a ruptured aneurysm, resulting in blood haemorrhaging into Chris's brain and killing him before they were able to get him into surgery, devastating Melissa.

It was irrational to think he'd abandoned her the way her parents had, but that was the way she felt, suddenly left to pick up the pieces of her life without him. She knew Lydia meant well organising this to get her out of the house, but she wasn't ready to move on. If she ever would be.

However, Lydia had gone to a lot of trouble. She was the only one who'd really been there for her, and Melissa reckoned she owed her. Even if it meant pretending to enjoy partying with a bunch of strangers in the rain.

'Come on then. We don't want to miss the headline act, do we?' She grabbed Lydia by the hand and pushed her way through the throng of people standing ankle-deep in mud until they had a good view of the stage. At least she knew a few of the band's songs so she wouldn't feel completely out of place.

In the end, Melissa was singing at the top of her lungs and dancing like everyone else. Temporarily forgetting her grief to lose herself in the moment. She had to admit, it felt good to be someone other than a bereaved fiancée for one day. Eyes closed, body swaying to the rhythm, she let go for once in her life. It was a feeling she could get used to.

'See? There is a party girl in there trying to get out. All we need now is to find you a man to remind you what else you're missing.' Lydia nudged her with her hip.

Sometimes Melissa wished she had her friend's confidence and outgoing personality. Lydia had already snogged three random blokes since they'd arrived and had indicated that she'd likely be sleeping somewhere other than their two-person tent tonight. She was someone who grabbed life with both hands and never wasted time on regrets or feeling sorry for herself. Melissa thought she should take a whole chapter out of her friend's book, but that didn't mean she was the sort of person to throw herself at a stranger.

'I'm not sure I'm ready for that, Lyds. Chris was the love of my life and I don't know if I want anyone else.' She couldn't imagine finding another man to replace Chris. Someone she could ever love as much as him.

Lydia rolled her eyes. 'I'm not talking about finding a husband. It's a music festival, Mel. I'm not sure the man of your dreams is standing waiting for you in this muddy field. But they do say the best way to get over someone is to get under someone else.'

Melissa couldn't stop her jaw dropping at the crass remark, watching agog as her friend pushed her way through to the makeshift bar at the side of the stage.

'Lydia! Chris isn't an ex who dumped me on a whim. He died.' The hysteria in her voice elevated that last fact to a level that stopped the bartender mid pour.

'I know that, Mel,' Lydia hissed through gritted teeth before flashing a smile at the man fixing their drinks. 'But the principle is the same. You have to move on, and it's okay to have a little fun with the opposite sex to do so.'

She handed Melissa a plastic glass containing some sort of orange-and-red concoction with a tacky paper umbrella sticking out of it. Melissa took a sip and winced. If this was what moving on tasted like, she wasn't sure she'd be overindulging.

'It's been so long, I wouldn't know what to do, even if I did meet someone.' If the time ever came when she was attracted to another man, didn't feel as though she was betraying Chris's memory by pursuing it, and didn't make a complete fool of herself in the process, it would be a miracle.

It was Chris who'd made the first move the night they'd met in the local pub. He'd made it clear he was interested in her, so she hadn't had to worry about being rejected, only that they'd be compatible. She'd never been like Lydia, brave enough to walk up to someone and let them know she was attracted to them. The few men she'd been with before Chris had come on to her, and, perhaps flattered by the attention, she'd ventured into relationships that were never going to work. It only added to her sense of not being worthy of love when they inevitably dumped her because she was a homebody, and they were still in party mode. She doubted meeting someone here was going to change that pattern, though Melissa definitely wasn't looking for a long-term commitment. The heartache and loss that inevitably followed the initial euphoria of meeting someone were things she could do without going through again.

Perhaps Lydia had the right attitude with her love-'em-and-leave-'em approach to dating. She certainly seemed like the happier of the two of them.

'It's like riding a bike,' Lydia said, aiming a wink at the handsome barman. 'You never forget.'

'Unless you never learned how...' Melissa grumbled.

'You shouldn't have to work too hard, Mel. You've got that glorious mane of red hair that makes you stand out in a crowd,' she said, undoing Melissa's ponytail to shake her tresses loose.

'And skin so pale it's liable to cause snow blindness.' She wasn't as fortunate as her honey-skinned, blond-haired companion who revelled in the sun when it made an appearance and wasn't forced to slather her entire body with factor fifty sun cream. A throwback to her Irish-born father's ancestors.

'You're a Celtic beauty. There's a guy by the burger van who certainly seems to think so. He hasn't taken his eyes off you in the last five minutes.' Lydia nodded somewhere over Melissa's shoulder as she sipped her drink through a straw.

Melissa almost broke her neck turning

around to see who might be interested in her. There was the usual crowd of inebriated posers trying to latch on to any woman who crossed their path, which Melissa definitely wasn't impressed by. She was about to tell Lydia so when someone caught her eye. A tall, handsome someone with short, dark hair and a cute smile.

He acknowledged her with a raised bottle of beer, and Melissa turned away with burning cheeks.

'He is kind of hot.'

In his white T-shirt and tight jeans, he looked like every other man here, but there was something in the twinkle of his eyes and the cheekiness of his grin that was hard to ignore. Not least because he seemed to be surrounded by a group of both men and women who were hanging on his every word.

'He looks like he could show you a good time.' Lydia shoved her forward, then resumed flirting with her barman.

Melissa turned her attention back to the man holding court with one eye on her. He was laughing as he swigged his beer, lifting the bottle up and dancing to the loud music coming from the main stage. Everyone near him seemed to be having the time of their lives. In fact, Melissa realised, she was the only one who wasn't.

Perhaps it was time for a change after all.

She was coming over. Lachlan's smile faltered as nerves got the better of him. It was one thing showing off and flirting, quite another following through with anything. He hadn't been with anyone since his ex, or his surgery.

'Looks like you've pulled, mate.' His brother Duncan muttered, watching the attractive redhead approach their group.

'I'm just here for the music, Dunc. To celebrate life.' He clinked his bottle to his brother's.

'And I'm glad you're still kicking, bro, but don't rule out relationships altogether. Just because things didn't work out with Julieann, it doesn't mean there isn't someone else out there for you.'

'There speaks the voice of a happily married man. Seriously though, if this is my second chance at life, I don't want to tie myself down. I intend to live my life to the fullest.'

It was okay for his brother, who had a wife and kids, and no cancer cells stealing away vital parts of his anatomy. But for Lachlan McNairn, staring death in the face had made him think about his mortality and the consequences it would have for those he left behind. He had grown up as the eldest in the family. When he was young, his dad had run away from his responsibilities and had left him to pick up the slack. He didn't want to be another absentee dad forcing the next generation to grow up too quickly in order to fill his role. As someone who'd given up his childhood, and a fair bit of his adulthood, to take care of his mother and siblings, he knew how unfair that was to ask of anyone.

Unfortunately, his ex hadn't seen his point. Family was still an important part of her future as far as she was concerned, so Lachlan had no other choice than to end their relationship. His treatment for testicular cancer had made it unlikely that it was still possible to have children. Even if he could have become a father, he didn't think it would've been fair at this stage to start a family. Not when there was always a chance of the cancer returning, perhaps more aggressively the next time.

So here he was, celebrating his recovery and the start of his new job as a paramedic in Glasgow. The next chapter of a life he hadn't been sure he'd get to experience. He certainly didn't need any complications of the romantic kind.

'Hey.' With the pretty dancer standing right in front of him, he promptly forgot all of that and went straight into flirt mode again.

'Hey.' She tucked a strand of hair behind her ear and fixed him with the most mesmerising pale blue eyes Lachlan had ever seen.

Suddenly the idea to spend this weekend at the festival getting drunk with his brother seemed a less attractive prospect than getting to know this woman.

'Lachlan.' He wiped the condensation from his beer bottle on his jeans and held his hand out.

'Melissa.' She shook it before he even had time to worry about how formal he was being, her smile reassuring him that he hadn't made a complete idiot of himself.

He was so out of practice when it came to being around the opposite sex. His experience was limited to his younger sister and Julieann, whom he'd been with since high school. Chatting women up wasn't something he'd had a lot of practice doing. When his teenage mates had been dating and going to parties, he'd been at home taking care of his siblings whilst his mum was at work. If he hadn't met his ex at the fast food restaurant he'd worked in to make extra cash to pay the family's bills, if she hadn't invited him out at the time, he might never have dated at all before his twenties. As it was, he'd only moved out of the family home once his little sister had grown up and sought her own independence. Now this was his time, and he was determined to make the most of it.

'Nice to meet you, Melissa. You seemed to be enjoying yourself in front of the stage earlier.' He'd been watching her dancing as though she hadn't a care in the world. Exactly how he wanted to feel. Preferably without the assistance of the toxic substances which most people here seemed to be taking to find that high. He'd had too many chemicals pumped into his body during his cancer treatment to even think about doing that. These days he didn't even drink more than a couple of beers because he didn't like that sense of being out of control of his body. Up close, he could tell Melissa wasn't under the influence of anything other than the determination to enjoy the atmosphere.

Her pale cheeks flushed a little pink, only

making her even more attractive. 'You saw that, huh?'

'Couldn't take my eyes off you.' Lachlan leaned in and spoke for her ears only. Even though Duncan was giving him some space, using the moment to phone his wife, Lachlan wanted to make sure his brother didn't hear. If he crashed and burned, he could do without the added humiliation of his brother witnessing it.

'I'm just here with my friend, Lydia.' Melissa glanced back at the voluptuous blonde draped over the bar.

'Special occasion?' He nodded towards the sparkly cowgirl hat. It wasn't really in keeping with the dark clothing she was wearing. Unlike her friend's leopard print, her navy maxi dress with a starry pattern wasn't shouting for attention. He wondered if she was part of a breakaway faction from a large hen party.

Melissa reached her hand up to her hat, as though she'd forgotten she was even wearing it. 'It's my birthday.'

'Happy birthday. Your twenty-first?' Very smooth.

She narrowed her blue gaze at him. Clearly not easily flattered. 'Thirtieth.'

'Ah. The thirties are the best years of your life.'

'Speaking from experience, are we?' Those pretty blue eyes twinkled with mischief.

'Well, the first ten months have been good.' Getting the all-clear from testicular cancer, moving to the city and bagging a new job was a pretty good start to his new decade. Even though he'd have to have regular check-ups and blood tests to make sure the cancer didn't return.

'Well, old man, how about buying me a birthday drink?' She tilted her chin up with the tease.

He liked her confidence, and she certainly wasn't being coy about what she wanted. Although Lachlan wasn't looking for anything serious with another woman, this festival was about celebrating a new chapter of his life. If that meant sharing it with a beautiful, fun-loving stranger, then he wasn't going to say no. He was looking forward to getting to know her a little better.

'I was just about to suggest that. Although perhaps we should move somewhere a little more grown-up.' As a group of lads near them bounced along to the music, beer spilling everywhere, Lachlan moved closer to Melissa, feeling protective.

'That would be nice. It's hard to talk when you can barely hear yourself think.'

They abandoned what was left of their drinks on one of the plastic tables in front of the burger van and began to walk away from the crowds.

'There's a pub across the road. If we're lucky, we might even get a seat to rest our thirty-year-old crumbling bones.' His grin was mirrored by Melissa, and he was glad she didn't seem to take herself too seriously. He didn't want to be with someone he'd have to tiptoe around. It was nice just to be himself, and have a laugh without any expectations.

Julieann had always wanted to talk about the future, settling down and having kids. Then there was Duncan. As much as he loved his brother, he'd spent most of this weekend listening to his marital problems or looking at pictures of his children. Some time kicking back with a drink and good company was exactly what he'd been looking for.

They were halfway across the field when the slight drizzle of the summer rain turned into a sudden downpour. Melissa let out a squeal and began running. He grabbed her hand and directed her towards the old concrete bus shelter at the edge of the road. Running and laughing, he felt like a teenager again. Or at least, he imagined this was how most teenage boys who hadn't had to grow up too quickly felt, hand in hand with a member of the opposite sex. Carefree, reckless... happy.

'I'm soaked,' she said through a bright grin as they sought shelter in the covered recess.

'No one else seems to be bothered. Are we wimps?' The rest of the festival-goers were still dancing, revelling in the rain and mud.

'I don't care. Give me a fire and a comfy armchair over that any day.' Melissa took a seat on the wooden bench with peeling red paint, and Lachlan sat down beside her.

'Add a hot toddy into that picture and I'm with you.' At this moment in time he couldn't think of anything better than sharing that cosy scene with her.

'Maybe some towels and a hairdryer too...' She tipped her head forward, sending a torrent of water running from her hat, then squeezed more out of the ends of her stunning russet hair.

He hadn't realised how drenched they'd got

in such a short space of time, and despite the mild temperature, Melissa was shivering.

'We'll make a run for it once there's a break in the rain.' Watching it from their hidey-hole was like being behind a waterfall, sheet rain sealing them off from the outside world.

He put his arm around her shoulders, attempting to generate some body heat through the thin fabric of the dress clinging to her body. Melissa looked up at him, gratitude shining in her eyes. Along with something else.

It had been so long he'd failed to recognise it at first. Attraction. Longing. Need. All the same things currently pulsing in his veins too. With the break-up, not to mention the cancer, sex had been the last thing on his mind for a long time.

Now, with Melissa looking at him with such undisguised yearning, he felt like the luckiest man on the planet. He leaned down and pressed his lips softly against hers, needing to touch her, taste her, and believe that she was real. That this stranger had appeared and awakened part of him he'd worried had been gone forever.

Melissa melted under Lachlan's touch. She'd forgotten how it felt to be with someone, how good it was to be wanted. For eighteen months, she'd been on her own, mourning the man she loved, forgetting to think of herself in the process. Lydia had been right—she still had a life to lead, and Lachlan was reminding her of that. She had needs, especially when this man was kissing her, slipping his arms around her waist and pulling her closer into his warm embrace. One night with him could help her move on and mark the start of this new decade in her life. Without Chris. She had to get used to the fact he was no longer part of her life, and with every tender kiss from Lachlan, he was gradually fading into the past.

It didn't mean she was ready to get into another serious relationship, but she doubted that's what would happen from hooking up with someone at a music festival anyway. Years from now, he would just be part of the special memories she was making celebrating her thirtieth birthday.

She kissed him back with an urgency that seemed to ignite more passion in him. Until things were getting pretty steamy in the sheltered nook. The sound of blood rushing in her ears, the feel of his strong hands anchored to her body, blotted out every last ounce of her usual common sense. So all that remained was the all-consuming need for more of Lachlan.

When he eventually wrenched his lips from hers, she was left dizzy and bereft.

'I think the rain is dying down. We should probably make a run for it. I have some towels and a hairdryer in my room you can use.'

'Room?' Her head still spinning from his passionate kisses, she thought she'd missed some vital piece of information.

'I'm staying over at the pub. It's cheating, I know, but there was no way I was sleeping in a tent in a field.' He looked shamefaced at the admission, but Melissa was only sorry she hadn't thought of the idea first.

'Sensible.'

'So, what do you say? We can go to my room and get dried off. No funny business, I swear.'

Melissa looked at the pub across the road, then at Lachlan as he took her hand. The feel of him there was both comforting and exciting, and she didn't want it to end when this was the most alive she'd been in months.

'Spoil-sport. I was looking forward to the funny business,' she said with a wink, pulling him behind her as she made her way across the road to the pub. Her pulse raced and her mouth was dry with the uncharacteristic attempt at seduction.

If she was going to convince Lachlan, and herself, that she was the type of woman who could have a one-night stand and walk away as if it never happened, she had to fake a Lydia-style confidence. Goodness knew that she didn't want to let this opportunity slip through her fingers. This was her chance to put the past behind her, just for one night, and she couldn't think of a more fun, exciting way to do it than spend it with Lachlan.

Lachlan's heart was beating a quickstep as they walked into the elevator. As much as he liked Melissa's forward nature, ruling out the chance of any misunderstanding or worry of rejection, he was a tad apprehensive. Not of Melissa, or what they were about to do, but more about his performance. Certain parts of him had been out of commission since his cancer treatment. Even though he'd likely never see Melissa again, he didn't want to let her down or embarrass himself.

He certainly hadn't felt sexy or virile during his treatment, more emasculated by it. It had taken a while, and some counselling, to come to terms with everything he'd been through. Though he'd had a reconstruction of the testicle he'd lost, he still knew a part of him was missing. Illogical though it was, sometimes he worried he was no longer the sexual being he used to be.

A fear that began to subside when she started kissing him once the elevator doors slid shut. Running the palms of her hands up his chest, pressing herself tightly against him, Melissa was leaving him in no doubt about how much she wanted him. The ultimate aphrodisiac, if it was needed.

When the elevator pinged open, they stumbled towards his room in a frenzy of kisses and searching hands desperate to keep hold of one another.

'Are you sure you want to do this?' he asked, as much for himself as Melissa. Did he really want to engage in meaningless, passionate sex with someone he'd only just met and wasn't likely to ever see again?

The answer from both parties was an overwhelming, breathless, 'Yes!'

He'd done the long-term thing, committed to someone and something which ultimately hadn't been right for him in the end. People and circumstances changed, so it seemed pointless to do it all over again with someone else he would probably end up disappointing eventually. At least this way there were no obligations or expectations beyond this room. And, if it did turn out to be a disaster, he wouldn't have to worry about facing her again. The beauty of being on this island was that people travelled from all over to be here. It wasn't as though they'd met at a local party in the park, where the potential for running into each other would always be a concern. Beyond first names, this was anonymous. Just for fun. The way he intended to approach the next part of his life.

Once she'd ditched her fetching headwear, he pulled her dress up over her head, uncovering her pretty lace underwear and sexy figure. Her skin was cool under his touch, goose pimples appearing as he slid her bra straps down her arms.

'Are you cold?'

Melissa bit her lip as she shook her head, indicating for the first time that she might be as nervous as he was about this.

'Burning up,' she replied, denying the hitch of apprehension in her voice.

It should have been a sign that perhaps this wasn't as casual as she wanted him to believe.

That she wasn't the sort of woman who could sleep with him and walk away without a second thought after all. Except he didn't want to heed that warning if it meant putting an end to this now. The urgency with which she stripped his shirt off obliterated any doubt. Everything in his body wanted more.

It was on the tip of his tongue to tell her he hadn't done this in a while, but that was personal, as were the reasons behind it. Rather than excusing himself before he let her down, he was hoping it wouldn't be too apparent. When she was touching him, kissing him, he certainly didn't feel as though he wasn't up to it. Where once he'd faced death, now he felt more alive than ever. He wished he could bottle this feeling.

Lachlan slowly undid Melissa's bra, uncovering her full breasts, which fit perfectly in his palms. She gasped as he kneaded the soft flesh and teased her pert nipples with his thumbs. So responsive and tempting. He dipped his head and sucked on the puckered pink tips until she was arching her body into his. He slid his hands into her panties and squeezed her round backside, pulling her flush against his ever-hardening body.

Melissa moved to unbutton his trousers,

and for a split second, he forgot he was anything other than a normal hot-blooded man. However, as she touched him through his boxers, he froze.

'Wait!' He backed away, putting some space between them.

'Have I done something wrong?' she asked, a worried look on her face. He cursed himself, and his illness, for putting it there.

'Not at all.' A one-night stand wasn't exactly the right situation for a deep and meaningful conversation. It wasn't easy to say that part of what made him a man was missing. Despite it being a recent event in his life, having a testicle removed wasn't something that cropped up in everyday conversation.

'You're married.' She sighed, folding her arms across her chest.

'No. I…er…just wanted to make sure this was what you wanted.' He decided it was worth the risk of letting her decide for herself if she still found him attractive or not. If he was ever going to get back in the dating game, he had to start somewhere, and Melissa was the first woman in an age he'd wanted to be with.

She hooked a finger into the waistband of his trousers and pulled him back towards her.

This time he didn't stop her from unzipping him, though he was tense as she touched him. The first person other than the doctor and surgeons who'd treated him who'd had access to that part of him. Thankfully this was a much more enjoyable experience.

Perhaps it was simply a man thing, thinking that he'd lost his masculinity somehow, or that Melissa would notice and find him less physically appealing. Someday he mightn't care so much, but since he was still coming to terms with what had happened himself, every rejection would hurt that much more.

He held his breath as she completely exposed him, taking him in hand and stroking him until he forgot everything except her touch. Her acceptance reinvigorated him, gave him more confidence, as he pulled her towards the bed with him.

He almost felt like the old Lachlan.

Melissa swallowed nervously as Lachlan covered her body with his. He was kissing her all over, being too considerate for what she needed. She didn't want someone making love to her, giving her reason to read more into this than was there. Hot, passionate sex was all she wanted, to fulfil a need and prove that she was able to move on.

She ground her hips against his, eliciting a groan from Lachlan.

'If you keep doing that, this is going to be over before either of us is ready.'

'Maybe I don't want to wait,' she said in her best sultry voice, grabbing his butt with both hands.

Another groan. Then he sank into her, locking their bodies together, and taking Melissa's breath away. Eyes closed, she gave herself over to the sensations he was awakening inside her.

Tonight, she'd let herself enjoy her freedom, the anonymity of a one-night stand, because tomorrow she had to go back to her real life. She'd be out of here the moment Lachlan was asleep, leaving him as nothing more than a wonderful memory.

CHAPTER TWO

Three months later

'NONE FOR ME, thanks.' Melissa held up her hand before Lydia could pour her a coffee. 'I'll just have a glass of water.'

'That's not going to keep you going through another shift. I hope you're not coming down with the same thing Lisa is out with.'

'Trust me, I don't think Lisa has what's ailing me,' Melissa mumbled, knowing she couldn't keep this to herself for much longer.

Lydia frowned, studying Melissa over her cup of coffee. 'Come to think of it, you haven't been yourself for a while. Not drinking after work, skipping your caffeine fix in the mornings. Are you on some sort of health kick?'

Melissa wished that's all that was stopping her from joining her work colleagues at the clinic in their usual weekend wind-down sessions at the local pub. Life would be so much simpler for her right now if she only had to worry about calorie counting. She was putting on a little extra weight, sure, but not because she'd been overindulging. At least not in food.

'There's something I have to tell you…' Her stomach rolled at the thought of saying it out loud. Once she admitted to it publicly, she had to face up to the fact that this was really happening.

She could see the second Lydia finally figured it out as her frown morphed into an expression of shock and horror.

'You're pregnant!'

Melissa nodded, the relief of finally sharing the news, and the enormity of how much her life was going to change, making her well up. She was tearful a lot these days, though her hormones might have had something to with it too.

'I'm pregnant. It took you long enough to work it out. And you're a midwife…' Melissa attempted to make light of it, though she'd been covering her tracks well since the positive test turned her life upside down. It was probably more out of denial than worrying about sharing the news before the end of her first trimester.

'I didn't know you were seeing anyone.'

'I'm not.'

'Then how? Oh…' Lydia's eyes were like saucers when the penny dropped. 'Festival guy?'

'Festival guy.' So much for slipping away and pretending it had never happened. Now she'd have a lifelong reminder of her reck- lessness.

Lydia pursed her lips. 'You're a midwife too. Did you forget how babies are made?'

Melissa deserved the sarcasm. It wasn't as though she hadn't beaten herself up over being so stupid.

'I know. I know. I was an idiot. When I was with Chris, I relied on the pill, and there hasn't been any need to take it since.' She and Lachlan had been too caught up in the passion of the moment to even think about contracep- tion at the time, and now she had to live with the consequences.

'Well, what's done is done. How do you feel about it?'

'I don't know. Chris and I had always planned to have a family someday, and when he died, I thought that dream was over. I want to be a mum, but my emotions are conflicted about the way it's happening. I mean, I'm on my own. In all those daydreams I had, I never imagined I'd be raising a child alone after a one-night stand.' Her parents, though not actively involved in her life these days, weren't likely to be impressed either. She hadn't seen much of them since they'd moved to America when she was eighteen. It had felt as though when she went to university she was no longer their responsibility. Their duty as parents was over.

Perhaps they'd imagined she didn't need them any more, but she hadn't suddenly become an independent, self-reliant adult simply because of a birthday. That was something she'd had to work on becoming in their absence, because they'd left her no choice.

Contact with them since had been limited, and the shame of getting pregnant by a stranger was liable to drive them even further apart.

Then there were the practicalities of being a single mum. She had no idea how she was going to juggle motherhood and a career. It was still all so overwhelming to try and get her head around.

'I take it the father doesn't know?'

Melissa just about managed not to laugh hysterically. 'I don't even know his surname, never mind anything else about him. Besides, it was supposed to be a one-night stand. A bit of fun to get over losing the love of my life. I think this goes way beyond casual sex.'

Even if she did know more about the father of her unborn child than his first name, she doubted she would get in touch. It would turn his world upside down too. Lachlan hadn't signed on for fatherhood, just a roll in bed.

If she was honest, not knowing anything about him was a good excuse to keep him out of the picture when she was still trying to come to terms with the situation herself. The guilt of betraying Chris's memory by having another man's child was already eating away at her conscience without having Lachlan in her life to remind her on a daily basis. In different circumstances she'd be married to the love of her life, both overjoyed at the prospect of starting their family. Living out their dream for the future with another man seemed to make a mockery of everything she and Chris had together. As though it had been easy to simply transfer those plans to someone else in his place. The reality was so different she wanted to weep, and had done so frequently since that first missed period. So much for no-commitment fun.

This pregnancy was a mistake, but she would raise the baby herself, and do her best to honour Chris's memory. That wouldn't happen with another man crowbarred into her life because of one moment of madness.

'These things happen. We both know that, Mel. You'll make a fantastic mother.' Lydia opened her arms out wide for Melissa and enveloped her in a hug.

'I hope so. I really hope so.' She let herself be comforted for a few moments. Then she thought about the women waiting for her, and pulled herself together.

'You know you can come to me anytime. I like the sound of Auntie Lydia…'

'Thanks. I'm probably going to need a babysitter, and a friend.' Lydia was going to be the fun auntie who'd spoil the little one rotten, and goodness knew Melissa and the baby were going to require some sort of support.

Lydia gave her an extra squeeze before releasing her. 'I'm not going anywhere.'

Melissa felt the tears welling again, and inhaled a shaky breath to fend them off. 'Right. I'd better go and see to the other pregnant ladies.'

She had appointments to keep with women who were looking to her for reassurance and guidance. There were another six months for her to fret over her own situation.

Melissa left Lydia in the staff room and headed to the small room she'd been allocated for seeing her patients. At least when she was working, she didn't have time for self-pity. It was her job which had saved her when Chris died, giving her a reason to get up in the morning and carry on, because these mothers-to-be were relying on her. As well as being the local community midwife, she often did shifts at the maternity wing in the hospital. She hoped her busy schedule would get her through this too and planned on working right up until the birth if possible. It was too scary to think about what would happen after that.

She pulled up her appointment list and patient files, glad to see Claire Burns was her first patient of the day. A chatty, friendly lady separated from her husband, and who was in the final days of her pregnancy. There was a comfort in knowing someone was in similar circumstances to Melissa's, that she'd gone through her pregnancy alone and hadn't fallen apart.

The knock on the door signalled her arrival.

'Come in,' Melissa called as she set out the

usual bits and pieces she needed for these antenatal checks.

'Hi, Melissa. I'm not on my own today.' Claire beamed as she walked in.

'Let me get another seat.' Melissa turned away to pull a chair over for the extra guest, hoping that she'd managed to reunite with her husband for a happy ending.

When she looked up and saw the man walking in, she almost keeled over.

'This is Lachlan. Lachlan, this is Melissa.' Claire introduced the man who'd put Melissa in her current predicament, and who she hadn't got out of her head in three months.

Lachlan held out his hand as the introduction was made, though he looked as shell-shocked as Melissa felt. 'Nice to meet you,' he said.

For obvious reasons, he apparently didn't want to acknowledge that they already knew each other.

Understatement of the year.

She managed to croak out a 'Hello.' Then almost collapsed into her chair, her body dealing with a mixture of emotions all at once.

Her initial reaction to seeing him had briefly been happiness, remembering the time they'd spent together and the thought that she'd never see him again. That was quickly followed by the realisation that he was here because he'd fathered someone else's baby. He'd lied to her when he'd said he wasn't married. Worse still, he'd walked out on his wife when she was pregnant. Clearly he wasn't the good guy she'd assumed him to be in the short time they'd spent getting to know each other.

'How've you been, Claire?' She tried to keep her mind on the job, ignoring the flush of colour she'd noticed in Lachlan's cheeks when he'd recognised her. He should feel embarrassed, sleeping with a stranger when he'd abandoned his own wife and child.

Her own blood pressure was rising as she attached the cuff to Claire's arm to check hers.

'Great, now that Lachlan's here for some support.'

The mother-to-be's smile made Melissa more nauseous than usual, seeing Claire fawn over a man who'd betrayed them both.

'Better late than never,' she mumbled, drawing a puzzled frown from her patient, reminding her to remain professional and set aside her personal feelings on the subject.

'Why don't you pop up onto the bed for me so we can check on baby's progress.' As Melissa pulled back the curtain from around the bed, she offered a bright smile to the couple.

Claire struggled to heave herself out of her chair, her huge bump clearly proving a hindrance these days. Lachlan stepped in and helped her up. Ever the gentleman.

Melissa took over, assisting her onto the bed, shooting Lachlan the darkest look she could muster. She didn't want to let him off scot-free. If she didn't get to speak to him privately and let him know what a lowlife she thought he was, she hoped she managed to convey it with one glance.

With a jerk of her hand, she pulled the curtain around the bed again, blocking out the sight of the man who'd unknowingly turned her life upside down.

Claire lay down and pulled her top up over her rounded tummy. 'I've been feeling a dull, heavy sort of ache, and she hasn't been squirming around as much as usual.'

After washing her hands, Melissa felt around Claire's bump, checking the baby's position. 'I think she's getting ready to come out. The head's engaged in the birth canal, so it shouldn't be long until you meet her for yourself.'

The sheer joy she saw on Claire's face at the news was something Melissa hoped she felt herself when it was her turn. By the time she was at this stage, she trusted she'd have got over the initial surprise and made preparations for her impending motherhood. For now, she was still somewhat in a state of shock over what had happened. Seeing Lachlan today, in these circumstances, wasn't going to help her get over it just yet.

'I can't wait. Lachlan's built the cot and decorated the nursery for me. I don't know where I'd be without him.'

Melissa resisted tutting or rolling her eyes as Claire sang his praises. It was the least he could do considering how much he'd upset Claire, leaving her to go through the pregnancy alone. Melissa supposed she was in the same position, though Lachlan was unaware of the other baby he'd fathered, and there would be no happy family for her at the end. Though she would do everything in her power to make sure her baby was loved enough for both parents. She knew all too well how it felt to be abandoned. Lachlan might not be privy to their child's existence, but she didn't suppose it would make any difference if he was. Someone who didn't stick around for a child inside a marriage surely wasn't going to be involved in raising one with a woman he barely knew.

She let Claire adjust her clothes, and tested the urine sample she'd brought with her. 'Everything looks good. I can't see you going far beyond your due date, so hopefully the next time I see you, you'll have your little girl in your arms.' That was the part she looked forward to most in her job. Although this one would be bittersweet, having to see Lachlan cooing over the baby. At least she'd be better prepared for running into him again in the future.

'I have my bag packed, all ready to go when the time comes.'

'And you have your birth plan… You might want to add your husband to that since you said you didn't want anyone with you in the delivery room.' When the time came, most women wanted a loved one with them, but Claire had been clear about doing it by herself because she'd have to get used to being on her own. Something Melissa admired and was thinking about adopting for her own birth plan. Although Lydia might have something to say about that one…

'What are you talking about? Why would I want to add my husband when I haven't seen him in months?' Claire was glaring at her, obviously upset by Melissa's comment.

Lachlan was scowling too, making it clear she'd messed up.

'Sorry. I just assumed Lachlan would want to be at the birth since he's here now.'

'Ew. Why would I want my brother at the birth?'

The room fell silent as the truth finally dawned on Melissa. She wanted to crawl into a hole and bury herself out of sight.

'Your brother?'

'Yes. He's just moved to the city, and he's been helping me get ready for the baby coming.'

'You thought I was the father? That I had walked out on a wife and unborn baby?' Lachlan was not as amused as Claire over the misunderstanding. His dark look indicated he wasn't happy that she saw him as someone who would easily abandon his family and sleep with a stranger.

'I—I'm sorry. My mistake.' In Melissa's defence, she didn't know him well enough to believe otherwise.

'No harm done,' Claire insisted, though Lachlan looked as though he was still brooding over the accusation. 'Actually, you might see more of my big brother from now on.'

'Oh?' Melissa's stomach was already swirling with the prospect of seeing him again in a professional capacity, pretending they didn't have intimate knowledge of one another. Their time together had been a one-off, out of character for her, but Lachlan wouldn't know that any more than she knew he was apparently the sort of man to step up and take care of his pregnant little sister.

'I've just started as a paramedic. Our paths might cross again from time to time,' Lachlan added, his jaw tense, giving an indication that he wasn't any more thrilled with the idea than she was.

'You've moved here? You're going to be working…here?'

His nod confirming her worst fears was all it took to start the room spinning.

Glasgow was a big city, but with her work as a local community midwife, they would be living and working in the same vicinity. Not to mention operating out of the same hospital. Something she hadn't anticipated when coming to terms with her future as a single mother.

'Melissa? Are you all right?' Claire's voice

sounded somewhere in the distance, but Melissa's head was whirring at the thought of Lachlan being in her life and the consequences of that.

A million thoughts and emotions overwhelmed her.

She never thought she'd see him again, and part of her had been sad about that when they'd had such a good time together. For a brief moment, she'd been happy he was more than a distant memory. The attraction she'd felt towards him was clearly still there. There was even the fleeting notion that she wouldn't be in this alone any more, that maybe Lachlan was going to be there for her and the baby. She would have the support in her life which had been missing for so long.

Now, however, the reality of him being here was beginning to sink in. It had been easy to relegate her time with him to the past, to focus on her future. The one she'd planned for her and her baby, without him. Letting him be part of that upended everything, and along with that reminded her of the betrayal of Chris's memory. Of course, the baby was always going to be evidence of that, but if Lachlan became a constant presence in their lives, there was a possibility he'd arouse more than feelings of guilt. After all, she'd liked him enough to sleep with him soon after their first meeting. She wasn't sure she wanted to run the risk of anything stronger than liking him developing.

It was probably safer to carry on as though he wasn't part of this.

There was no way she'd be able to hide her pregnancy forever. If he saw her again over the course of the next few months, it wouldn't take much for him to figure it out.

Her acceptance of her situation was in jeopardy now that everything appeared to be spinning wildly out of control. This wasn't how she'd planned things. She'd been preparing to do this alone and hadn't counted on ever seeing or dealing with him again.

Melissa felt as though she was being buried alive by the skeletons tumbling out of her closet.

She stumbled, grabbing for the desk, closing her eyes in an attempt to regain her composure.

Strong hands were suddenly holding her up, guiding her into a chair. A familiar deep voice asking if she was okay. One she heard in her dreams at night. Perhaps she was still asleep and this was a nightmare, all of her worst fears come true.

'Melissa? Should I get someone?' There it was again, that voice which had sweet-talked her into bed and changed her life forever...

It took her a moment to remember where she was and who else she was with.

'No. I'm fine.' She shook Lachlan off. It wasn't going to help her gather her composure if he was touching her, reminding her of the last time they'd been in close contact.

'Are you sure? You're looking a little green.' Lachlan's concern only irritated her and made her more determined to get rid of him.

'I skipped breakfast this morning. I'm sure it's just low blood sugar making me a little light-headed. I'll be sure to grab something to eat from the staff room before the next patient comes in.'

'It's the most important meal of the day, so they say. Although I couldn't face it in the early days of my pregnancy with the morning sickness. You're not pregnant are you, Melissa?' Claire laughed, and the best thing Melissa could have done was laugh it off too, but she couldn't, because there was nothing funny about it.

She just froze. Trapped in the headlights of the truth.

'Melissa?'

She could hear the unspoken question in Lachlan's voice, feel his eyes burning into her. What she said next could affect both of their lives forever.

There was nothing to be gained from telling him now except a whole lot of disruption for both of them. Lachlan was clearly starting some new stage of his life too. The last thing either of them needed was to be thrown together, forced to co-parent for the rest of their lives. She knew nothing about him, and though she should have thought about that much earlier, she'd learned her lesson. There was more than herself to worry about now.

'Very funny.' She gulped down the truth and tried to pass Claire's question off as a joke.

'Ignore me,' Claire said. 'I've obviously got babies on the brain at the minute.'

'No worries. It's understandable when you're getting close to your due date, but everything looks good, Claire. I'll make another appointment to see you, but hopefully you won't need it.' Melissa scribbled down the date and time on Claire's appointment card, in a hurry for the two to leave. She had a lot to process and needed some time on her own before she saw her next patient.

'I'll see you soon.' Claire got to her feet with her brother's assistance, and Melissa was ready to breathe a sigh of relief as they moved to the door.

With both of them working in the medical field in the same city, it was possible Lachlan would find out the truth anyway. She'd panicked being on the spot like that, but Lachlan hadn't questioned anything. In fact, he barely acknowledged her as he walked out the door, so perhaps she was worrying about nothing.

Melissa was shaking when they finally left. It had been a close call, but she hoped Lachlan was out of her life for good this time.

'She's lovely, isn't she?' Claire was extolling the virtues of her midwife, but Lachlan's mind was firmly trained on the woman he'd watched dancing in the mud, and kissed in the rain. He'd never believed he'd get to see her again. Especially since she'd ghosted him in the middle of the night, disappearing without a trace, except for the smile she'd left on his face.

And now that Claire had suggested Melissa might be pregnant, he couldn't get the thought out of his head. Was it his imagination, or was there a certain roundness in her curves that hadn't been there before? A glow that suggested perhaps it wasn't beyond the realm of possibility, despite her dismissal of Claire's comment.

Melissa hadn't directly denied the suggestion she might be pregnant, and she'd hesitated just a fraction too long. Ordinarily, she would have every right to keep that sort of information to herself. She wasn't obliged to share private matters with her patients. However, her reaction upon seeing him only raised more red flags. He could understand seeing a one-night stand in the workplace would be embarrassing for her, but she'd almost passed out when they'd come face-to-face and she'd learned he'd moved to the city. It gave the impression there was something more going on than regret.

What if it was his baby and she'd simply been afraid of talking to him about it in front of Claire?

Neither Duncan nor Claire knew anything about their tryst at the festival. When his brother had queried his sudden disappearance, he'd simply put it down to having too much to drink and going to sleep it off.

In hindsight, he and Melissa hadn't used any protection, but with his medical history, he hadn't imagined the chance of anyone conceiving his baby after one night was very high. It was still possible, though, and he needed to know for sure. Although becoming a father wasn't something he wanted, he wasn't going to abandon a child the way his own dad had readily done with his whole family.

Whatever the truth, he had a feeling Melissa was going to be a part of his life here in Glasgow. And the idea wasn't as scary as it should've been.

CHAPTER THREE

'AM I GLAD to see you. I had visions of having to deliver this baby myself.' An anxious-looking husband opened the door for Lachlan and his colleague.

'I'm Lachlan, the paramedic.'

'Gordon. The husband.'

He shook hands with the man, who looked as though he was about to start hyperventilating at any moment.

'What's your wife's name?'

'Marie. She's upstairs in the bedroom.'

'And there's no sign of the midwife arriving anytime soon?' Although they were absolutely the people to call in an emergency, when it came to births, that was the midwives' department. Lachlan and his colleagues only got involved when there was no other option. Like now.

'She's caught up in traffic and told us to call

for you in case she didn't get here in time. I don't think this baby is going to wait.'

'Okay, well, we'll see how things are looking.' Lachlan made his way to the bedroom, with the husband close behind.

'Hi, Marie. I'm Lachlan. I understand baby seems to be in a hurry. Was this a planned home delivery?' he asked the woman.

She nodded through panting breaths. 'Although we hadn't counted on a storm preventing our midwife from getting here on time.'

'I understand, and if she gets here soon, we'll certainly hand over your care into her capable hands. For now, though, I need to see how far labour is progressing, okay?' These days home births weren't uncommon. Sometimes going through labour in the comfort of their own homes, in familiar surroundings, made the birthing experience that bit more pleasant for mums. It could certainly be a calmer atmosphere than being under the fluorescent lights in a busy hospital ward, without the sound of machines, babies crying, and the general chatter. As long as they had support from their familiar midwives and hadn't been forced to call in the emergency services last minute.

Though Lachlan would do his best not to

show it, he was anxious about the possibility of having to deliver this baby. It was a big responsibility, bringing a baby into the world, and was something he'd only done in theory until now.

'There's another one coming,' Marie managed through gritted teeth, sitting up in bed as the next contraction hit.

'Just breathe through it. We can wait until it passes. Deep breaths. In and out…' Lachlan took her hand and breathed with her, ignoring how hard Marie was squeezing, until the contraction began to subside.

Once it had passed, and the circulation was back in his fingers, Lachlan went to wash up so he could examine her.

'If you can slide your feet up and let your knees fall open, I'm just going to see how you're progressing.' He had hoped since this was her first baby that they might have enough time to transfer her to the hospital so they could deliver there, but it soon became apparent that wasn't going to be an option.

'You're almost fully dilated. It looks as though we're going to be welcoming baby soon.'

Marie looked relieved, but when Lachlan

felt around her bump, there was more cause to be concerned.

'When you had your scans at the hospital, was there any indication that the baby might be in the breech position?'

'No. Why? What's wrong?' Marie grabbed for her husband's hand, understandably distressed that things weren't going according to plan.

'Okay, I don't want you to panic, but baby seems to have moved position. He's coming out feet first.' Lachlan tried to keep his voice calm as he delivered the information, not wanting to upset his patient. Even though he was feeling the pressure even more.

A breech birth made things trickier for him without the usual resources of the hospital should he need them.

'Is everything going to be all right?' Marie's husband asked.

'Yes. Baby's heartbeat is fine, but his position will just make the delivery a little trickier. Everything will be okay. We need to keep Marie calm and relaxed until then. You're both doing great.' Lachlan gave them his best optimistic smile, despite his heart trying to beat its way out of his chest.

Marie nodded and squeezed her husband's

hand a little tighter when another contraction took over. Once it had passed, Lachlan was able to offer some pain relief. He needed the mother to be relaxed for the next stage.

When they heard the knock on the front door, there was a collective sigh of relief.

'That'll be the midwife.' Marie's husband rushed downstairs to let her in, Lachlan thankful his prayers had been answered.

'I'm so sorry. The storm brought down a few trees blocking the roads. I got here as soon as I could.' Melissa bustled into the room looking more than a little windswept as she shrugged off her coat.

'It's no problem. Marie's fully dilated, and baby is in the breech position.' Lachlan was glad to have her here for a multitude of reasons. The most pressing was the imminent birth, but on a personal level, he was happy to have another opportunity to speak to her. He hoped after this was over, they'd get a chance to talk about the time they'd spent together, so it wouldn't be the elephant in the room every time they did come into contact.

'Okay.' Melissa rolled up her sleeves and examined Marie for herself. When she'd got the call about Marie's labour starting, she hadn't expected to walk into this.

A breech birth was one thing—she could handle that—but she hadn't been prepared for Lachlan being on the scene too. Since seeing him again at his sister's appointment, Melissa had had a crisis of conscience about whether or not she should have told him about the baby. She was still undecided as to what action to take, but perhaps spending some time with him tonight would tell her more about his character and point her in the right direction. His job as a paramedic was a responsible one, as proven tonight by him taking charge in her absence. He'd also shown maturity in helping his sister out. The voice that had been nagging her about doing the right thing was telling her these were the sorts of qualities needed in a father figure. She simply wasn't sure if she was ready to have him in her life.

A conversation was definitely needed, but for now, her patient was the priority.

'When you feel the next contraction, I want you to push, okay?'

Marie nodded, and her husband mopped the sweat from her brow with a cold washcloth. Giving birth was very much on the mother, but those fathers who chose to be there for it generally did their best to help. Keeping their partners calm and offering support might not seem like a lot in the circumstances, but she knew it could make all the difference to a frightened woman.

It made her think about her own labour. She hadn't written her birth plan because she didn't want to think about it, or how lonely she would be. Even if Lydia volunteered herself to be her birthing partner, it was never going to be the same as having a significant other with her. Knowing she'd have someone to take her and the baby home, someone to share the responsibilities with. She supposed as long as the baby was healthy, that was all that mattered, but it didn't mean she wouldn't be a little down in the circumstances.

When she'd thought about starting a family, she'd imagined it would be with Chris. That he would be as excited and as anxious as she was about becoming a parent and meeting their baby for the first time. It wasn't the same falling pregnant to a stranger she knew nothing about.

Even if she confessed to Lachlan that he was the father, and he wanted to be there for the birth, it wasn't going to be the cosy family she'd always pictured. Worse still, she might come to hope for that possibility if Lachlan was on the scene, and she couldn't risk her heart on what could be a wasted exercise. Letting him into her life at all was leaving her vulnerable. She would have to remember that if Lachlan did want to be part of his baby's life, it would be because he felt obligated, not out of love. For her, that was the most important thing about being a parent. It wasn't something to go into half-hearted, because the child would feel it. She knew how it felt to be an afterthought.

It would be safer to keep Lachlan on the outside, but she knew it wasn't fair to leave him in the dark. The decision about whether or not he would be a father should be Lachlan's, not hers.

'Here we go again...' Marie gripped her husband's hand and bore down as the contraction took hold.

Melissa helped her breathe through the contractions until she saw the baby emerging.

'Okay, Marie, I need you to take it easy. It's best for baby to make his own way out now.' The hands-off approach wasn't something that came naturally to her, but letting the baby deliver itself in this situation was the best option to prevent any further problems.

Hopefully in this case, the only reason they would need transferred to the hospital would be for mother and baby to have a welfare check.

'Good, Marie. Just hold off on pushing for me so baby can come out himself.'

Melissa concentrated on catching the baby as he slipped quietly from his mother. Then she moved quickly to cut the umbilical cord and clean him up.

'Why isn't he making any sound?' Understandably, Marie voiced her concern.

'Sometimes babies need to adjust to their new surroundings.' Melissa didn't want to panic just yet. She knew the procedures. On occasion, babies were stunned by their sudden emergence into the world and needed their airways cleared or a little assistance before they started breathing on their own. She could feel the eyes of everybody in the room burning into her, relying on her to save this baby's life. Or start it.

'Lachlan, can you grab the aspirator from my bag, please?'

Without a trace of panic, or the slightest hesitation, Lachlan placed the tiny mask over the child's mouth and nose, squeezing some air into his lungs. The pressure was even greater than usual when they weren't in a hospital setting, and failing here didn't just mean embarrassing herself. It meant the loss of a child. She was in charge, but Lachlan was such a confident and assured paramedic, she couldn't have asked for better backup in a potentially tragic emergency. This wasn't his field of expertise, but he wasn't afraid to step up when he was needed.

There was absolutely no reason she shouldn't tell him about his baby, except for her own issues over it.

When the newborn's chest started to rise and fall, there was a collective sigh of relief around the room, and tears from the new parents.

'Is he all right?' Marie asked as Melissa handed her son to her for the first cuddle.

'He's fine, but given the circumstances, it's best you both go to the hospital to get checked over. Lachlan will take you in the ambulance, and I'll follow in my car.'

'Can I hold him?' Gordon asked, clearly keen to meet his son.

'Of course. Why don't you take him for now whilst I get Marie ready for transfer.'

Marie carefully handed over her precious cargo to her husband. 'Watch his head. Make sure you've got him.'

'I've got him,' he assured her, the look of love in the man's eyes for his son making Melissa want to weep. Not only because it was such a lovely moment seeing him meet his child for the first time, but because she was preventing her baby from having the same welcome into the world from their father.

'Congratulations. We'll wait outside until you're ready to leave.' Lachlan and his colleague discreetly left the room, leaving her to deliver the afterbirth and ensure Marie was all right to be transferred to the hospital.

He gave her a smile and a nod before he disappeared out the door, and in that moment, her heart ached to tell him her secret. Despite not wanting to invite Lachlan further into her life, afraid of getting close to anyone again, she knew she couldn't deny him the chance of being a father to his own child.

Telling Lachlan he was the father of her baby left both of them open to hurt and rejection, but it was something she knew she had to do. What happened after that would be entirely down to him.

* * *

'You don't have to stay, you know,' Melissa said to Lachlan as he waited for news on mother and baby.

'It's fine. My shift's over. I just wanted to make sure they were all right. My first breech birth.' Not that he'd been actively involved in the end. Though he'd been ready to deliver the baby, he'd been relieved when Melissa had turned up to take over.

She'd been amazing, keeping her patient calm, and talking her through what was going to happen. Again, when the baby hadn't been breathing. It had been a scary time for everyone in that room, but Melissa hadn't once given anyone reason to panic. He'd been in awe of her.

Melissa smiled. 'Birth is an amazing thing.'

'So are you.' He hadn't known the words were going to leave his head and make their way out of his mouth, but they were true nonetheless.

It would have been easy to write Melissa off as some hippy-dippy free spirit from their first meeting at the festival, but she was far from that. She was a strong, capable woman who clearly didn't need him in her life. But Lachlan couldn't help being drawn to her. The memory of their time together at the festival hadn't left him, and wasn't likely to now that he was getting to know her a little better.

Since his cancer treatment, he hadn't thought much about getting into another relationship. But if he ever did, he imagined it would be with someone like Melissa. They'd had a connection from the first moment they'd met, and nothing since had made him feel any differently. Except he didn't want anything serious. The intensity of these last months during and after his treatment had left him emotionally and physically exhausted. He didn't have room for anything more in his life right now. Even if Melissa was interested in him as anything other than a fellow medical professional.

'I think we need a cup of tea and a debriefing… I mean, a chat about what happened. Even I don't see that many spontaneous breech births.' Melissa went a little pink, and Lachlan knew she was thinking about their night together too. The last time they'd *debriefed*.

'Yeah, it's been one hell of a night.' Despite being aware of all the reasons he should say no and go home, he couldn't resist the chance to spend a little more time with her. He didn't know a lot of people in the city yet, and he was already aware of what great company she was. Okay, so they weren't likely to pick up where they'd left off, but it didn't mean they couldn't talk to one another at least.

Melissa led the way towards the canteen with Lachlan following, wishing it was a pub they were heading to instead.

The servery was closed, but the vending machines and seats were still available, so they waited for their paper cups to fill with what passed for tea and went to sit down.

'I'm glad you were there tonight,' Lachlan said honestly. Although he would've done his best for mother and baby, there was no one as experienced as the midwives when it came to delivering babies. Especially in circumstances like tonight when complications arose.

'I think you were doing okay on your own.'

'As I said, I'm glad you were there.' He took a sip of the tea, wishing it was something stronger. Both of their jobs had a high level of responsibility. People's lives were in their hands. But when it came to newborn babies, the pressure was so much greater. They were innocent souls just embarking on life. He didn't want to imagine how it would feel to lose one.

'So, you moved here to be with your sister?' Melissa shifted past the work stuff to the personal questions, but he supposed it was only natural for her to be curious about why he was here. Neither of them had expected to cross paths again.

'Partly. I needed a new start, and when this position came up, it also meant I could be here for Claire when the baby came. She doesn't have anyone else around her.'

'Won't your parents help out?'

'Mum lives out in the country and works in a farm shop. She doesn't want to move to the city, and Dad left when we were little. I barely remember anything about him, other than the mess he left us in. Mum had two jobs to keep a roof over our heads, and as the eldest, I pretty much raised my brother and sister. What about you? Have you got family here?'

Melissa shook her head, a sadness seeming to fall over her. 'No. They're living in America. Have done since I was eighteen.'

'You've been on your own all this time?'

'Yup. I don't have a lot of contact with them at all. I put myself through my midwife training and supported myself financially.'

'You're a strong woman, Melissa. You should be proud of yourself.' Lachlan didn't mean to be patronising, but if she didn't have her parents around, he supposed no one told her that very often.

'I'm not so sure about that. There are some things I'm not proud of. You know, seeing Marie and Gordon back there has given me some food for thought. There's something I need to tell you.'

Lachlan's heart was hammering against his ribcage as he waited for the response. He wasn't sure he was ready to hear whatever she had to say.

The way her gaze was locked onto his as though she was trying to communicate something telepathically rather than actually saying it out loud didn't help his anxiety.

'I'm pregnant.'

'Oh. Congratulations.' In that moment, he didn't know what else to say. He wondered why she was telling him now.

Melissa hung her head and let out a sigh, looking incredibly guilty about something. It occurred to him that she might have been in a relationship when they got together and was now remorseful, or worried he'd tell someone.

'If you're with someone, it's okay. I won't say anything about us.'

She took a gulp of tea before she spoke.

'I'm not with anyone, Lachlan. I haven't been with another man since the festival. In fact, you're the only man I've slept with in nearly two years.'

It took a moment for him to process what she was saying. The enormity of those few words eventually floored him. There was so much wrapped up in that night they'd spent together. It was always going to be more than a casual thing. Although he didn't know the details of Melissa's personal life, they'd clearly both been going through an emotional time. If she wasn't the sort of woman to sleep around, then he wondered what had prompted her to do so with him. He'd been breaking free from his old life, hoping to start all over again. Melissa must've had her reasons too.

'So…' He wanted her to spell it out for him.

'You're the father of my baby.'

'But you didn't say anything—'

'I know. I was surprised to see you that day. Claire put me on the spot, and I hadn't thought about how I was going to tell you. I didn't think I'd ever have to.'

Lachlan was sure that his spirit had left his body, that the shock of the information had killed him where he was sat. He was numb, the breath whooshing out of his lungs.

'I'm the father. Of your baby.' It wasn't so much a question, but a confirmation of what she'd told him so it might actually sink in. His one-night stand had suddenly turned into a lifetime commitment. However long that may, or may not, be.

'Yes.'

'And you wouldn't have told me if I hadn't walked into your office that day?'

She looked away. 'I didn't know anything about you. If I recall, that was the point of our time together.'

'I think having a baby negates the usual rules of a one-night stand.' He could feel the anger building inside him, replacing the shock. Melissa hadn't even been prepared to give him the chance of being a father. Okay, so it wasn't something he had planned for, but he suspected neither had she. He had the right to know she was carrying his baby and at least be given the option of getting involved. They'd conceived this child together, after all.

'I didn't even know your surname, Lachlan. I still don't.'

'McNairn. I'm sure you would have found me eventually if you'd tried.' It was clear she'd had no intention of telling him. He wondered what would have happened if he hadn't moved to Glasgow. The fact that he could have had a child out there that he'd never known about, all while thinking it wasn't possible for him to be a parent, seemed cruel. Of course, Melissa wasn't aware of his medical history, but it had still taken her until now to tell him, knowing he was in the city. He couldn't help but take that personally.

'It was quite a lot for me to get my head around too, Lachlan. My friend Lydia dragged me to the festival to celebrate my thirtieth birthday. It was supposed to help me get over the death of my fiancé, Chris, twenty-one months ago.'

'I'm sorry. What happened?' That went some way to explaining why she'd kept the news to herself. Getting over her loss would've been no small thing.

He'd been right in his assumption that their time together had been more than a casual hookup for her too. Especially if it had taken her this long to even try to move on.

'It was sudden. A brain aneurysm, they said.' There was a faraway look in her eyes, as though she was reliving the moment, and he could see the terror and pain residing within her.

It was the same look he'd seen on the faces

of his family when he'd been going through his treatment. But his story had a happier ending. For now.

'That must've been horrific for you.' He reached out and took her hand to comfort her, the first contact they'd had since meeting again. Her skin was as soft and warm as he remembered.

She tried to smile through the tears filling her eyes, but her quivering bottom lip gave away her sadness. 'We'd planned to get married and have a family of our own. When he died, I thought that dream was over, so discovering I was pregnant after our night together was as big a shock to me as it is to you now. I'm still coming to terms with it.'

He was beginning to understand her motive for not coming clean sooner. Melissa, despite first impressions, was the settling down kind, and she'd realised pretty quickly that wasn't what he was interested in. Far from bringing a baby into a loving, established relationship, she was facing being tied to a man who'd picked her up at a music festival. And that was before she even knew he was someone who'd already had cancer once, and wasn't guaranteed to be around long-term. The question was where they went from here.

He didn't want to scare her away by revealing his own health problems when she'd already been through so much.

'Why tell me now then?' He needed to know her motives for wanting him involved before he committed himself to anything. He didn't want to be another useless father like his own, or his brother-in-law, but he also needed to know she wasn't going to shut him out again if a better prospect came along.

Melissa was still holding his hand, so he took that as a good sign. 'I can tell you're committed to Claire and her baby.'

'Of course. She's my little sister. I've been looking after her for most of her life, and I want to make sure her child hopefully has the positive role model in their life that we didn't. I'll do my best to support them.'

'See. You're a good brother. I felt bad about not telling you the other day, but I was afraid of what it would mean for me to let you into my life. Then I saw you with the family tonight and realised I had to tell you. It's not fair to keep you out of the baby's life for my own selfish reasons. Now that you know, I'm hoping you'll make a good father too. Though it's entirely down to you if you want to be involved or not.'

'I want to be, if you'll give me the chance.' It was asking a lot of both of them, expecting Melissa to put her faith in him, and for him to commit to a family he never wanted.

'Claire's going to get a bit of a surprise, isn't she?' Melissa broke the tension with a smile, and a reminder that this wouldn't affect just the two of them.

'Have you told your parents?'

'Not yet.' Keeping this to herself for months went to show how much she'd been struggling with the news herself, but from now, on she wouldn't have to cope on her own.

'At least you know the name of the father of your unborn baby now.'

'Not funny, Lachlan,' she said, letting go of his hand to swat him on the arm, but she did so with a smile. They were making progress.

'Seriously, though, tell me what you want from me, Melissa. We're in this together.' He'd be lying if he said he didn't feel sick, that his gut wasn't churning with the prospect of becoming a father, and what that meant for the future. But they were both responsible for the situation they were in, and he'd never been one to walk away from his responsibilities.

'I'm not expecting anything from you, Lachlan. If you don't want to be involved, I'll understand.' Melissa was saying the words, but Lachlan wasn't sure she meant them. From everything else she'd said, he got the impression she was worried about going through this on her own, and he wasn't going to let her.

'I'm here. I'm involved. I'm the father.' Something he was going to have to repeat to himself until it finally sank in too.

'I've got my three-month scan coming up soon, if you'd like to be there?'

'I would.' Then finally they would both have to face the reality of the situation. When they saw their baby on the screen, there would be no denying this was happening, that it was more than just words and worries about the future. They'd created a life. One which they were both responsible for.

Only time would tell if they were up to the task ahead.

CHAPTER FOUR

'THANKS FOR DOING THIS,' Melissa said as they parked up outside the hospital.

It hadn't been easy facing Lachlan again after breaking the news that he was the father of her baby. Even less so having to ask him for a lift because she'd been feeling nauseated this morning.

'It's no problem.' Lachlan flashed her a smile, which she probably didn't deserve after almost denying him the chance to be a father.

'I just didn't want to take the chance of driving up here on my own and taking ill. It's probably nothing more than nerves, but I thought maybe I should have some company.' It had crossed her mind to go to Lydia first. She would have been the safer option, but Lachlan knew the scan was today, and it would've seemed churlish not to include him. Especially when he'd been hurt by her keeping the pregnancy to herself until now.

All things considered, he'd taken the news well. She'd dropped a baby bomb right in the middle of his world, and a lot of men would've gone running in the opposite direction. Not Lachlan.

'I told you I would be here for the scan.'

'You did.' Although she hadn't been one hundred percent sure he'd meant it, and a part of her had hoped he might not turn up. It would've made things easier for her if Lachlan decided he didn't want to get involved after all. Then she could just get on with things on her own the way she'd planned. Without worrying about having Lachlan in her life and the complications that brought.

Lachlan got out of the car and came around to open her door for her. 'Claire's excited about having a playmate for her little one.'

'You told her?' She couldn't help but wince at how that conversation might have gone.

It didn't make her look very professional getting pregnant by a patient's brother, even if they'd both been oblivious to the connection, or the consequences, at the time.

'Of course. I've told all the family, and they're thrilled. Although, to quote Claire, she doesn't know what you see in a "numpty" like me.'

That made her laugh. It was funny how grown adult siblings resorted to their childish selves when they were together. Chris and his brother used to engage in wrestling bouts at family get-togethers, and Lydia and her sister still fought like teenage girls over clothes and boys. Sometimes it made her glad she'd been an only child, but other times, like this, she wished she had that sort of bond with another family member.

It made her wonder about their baby, and if it would ever have a brother or sister in the future. If she could be in a stable, loving relationship where she would even think about having another baby. She certainly wasn't going to accidentally get pregnant with another stranger to do so. It was too emotionally complex and taxing.

'I told her, I'm handsome, fun, and currently looking after two pregnant ladies. I'm an absolute catch,' Lachlan joked, though every word was true. That was the problem. The very reason she was wary about opening up her life to let him in, if there was the smallest chance he would leave her the way everyone else in her life had.

It was plain to see that he had a special bond with his sister, teasing one another, but close all the same. Perhaps that was part of the reason she'd always wanted to have a family of her own. To have that security around her, ensuring she'd never be on her own again. Obviously, things hadn't worked out that way, and though she was happy she was going to have a child to share her life with, it was unfortunate she couldn't provide her offspring with the family she didn't have. Of course, Lachlan was going to be involved on some level, but it wasn't the same as having two loving parents raising their child in the same house. The chances of her having any more children to give this baby siblings were very low too, since this pregnancy hadn't been planned.

She supposed she should get used to feeling this level of guilt, since it seemed to be part of being a parent. Always worrying about doing the right thing for your child, and blaming yourself when things weren't perfect.

'Well, I'm grateful for your support, but I hope you've told her we're not a couple.' Melissa didn't want any misunderstanding on anyone's part. There was no way of knowing how things were going to play out in the future, but there was little point in getting carried away by the idea they were all going to end up being one big happy family.

'Yes. Although it was mortifying having to explain the circumstances.'

She could only imagine, and was glad she hadn't been there at the time, facing judgement of their reckless behaviour at the festival.

'Listen, I'll understand if you don't want to be here, or if you have something else to do. There'll be more scans for us to attend together. Or not. Whatever you decide.' Melissa didn't want to make things difficult for him, forcing him to be here if he wasn't one hundred percent on board. She hadn't left him much choice today when he'd had to drive her.

'Why would I want to miss seeing my baby for the first time? I thought you wanted me to be here.' A scowl marred his handsome features as they made their way towards the waiting room, and she knew immediately she'd said the wrong thing.

'I do, but I know you didn't ask for this. I'm giving you a way out.' She knew once they saw the baby together on the screen, there would be no going back for either of them.

Lachlan turned and fixed her under his dark glare. 'I said I'll be there, and I will.

If this is your way of trying to push me out again, it's not going to work. This is my baby too, whether we like it or not.'

Far from being reassured by the statement, Melissa was reminded that he didn't want to be here at all. His involvement was merely because he felt a duty. She'd changed her mind about telling him about the baby after Marie's delivery because it was good to have his support and know he was there if she needed him. It made her think about her own labour, and if anything went wrong how nice it would be to have someone there with her. However, she didn't want that to be under sufferance. That wasn't how she wanted to welcome her baby into the world. It would be better to be on her own in that scenario in a room full of love, rather than regret and reluctance.

The shine of the afternoon was tarnished by Lachlan's words, her excitement at seeing her baby on the screen overshadowed by the thought that she'd strong-armed Lachlan into being here. That had never been her intention, but she couldn't help but worry that he didn't really want to be part of this. He was just the kind of man who felt compelled to step in when he was needed. Perhaps that was enough for some women, but Melissa would have preferred that he had a real emotional connection to their baby. With parents who acted sometimes as though she didn't exist, she didn't want the same for her child.

If Lachlan was only on the scene because he felt a duty to be there, there was always a chance he could walk away too. Without any emotional attachment to her or the baby, it was only that sense of responsibility keeping him here. And goodness knew it hadn't been enough for her own parents to stick around forever. One day he might decide to follow dreams that didn't include being tied down to a child he'd never wanted, and then where would she be if she'd already made room for him in her life? Alone, wounded, and with a baby to take care of on her own. Exactly why she'd been reluctant to tell him in the first place. At least then she'd be doing this alone by choice, without having further reason to feel abandoned.

They sat in silence in the waiting room, an empty chair filling the distance between them. A stark comparison to the happy couples around them holding hands and chattering excitedly as they waited to see their babies.

'Melissa Moran?'

When her name was called, she got up and walked away without even looking to see if Lachlan was following her. She couldn't bear to see any trace of resentment on his face.

The sonographer checked her details, then asked her to get up onto the bed. It was the first time she'd looked at Lachlan since she'd been called, and was surprised to find him already sitting by the bed, watching the screen. Perhaps he wasn't as disinterested as she'd convinced herself he was.

'Can you just pop your top up over your belly for me, Melissa, and pull the waistband of your skirt down a little bit?'

Melissa acquiesced, and the sonographer tucked some paper towel down the front of her skirt. 'It's just so we don't get any gel on your clothes.'

It was odd being on the other side this, when she was usually the one issuing instructions to anxious mothers-to-be. She'd have to get used to it with six months of her pregnancy to go. Although it would probably help her empathise more with her patients in the future. Their worries, and the extra problems pregnancy caused in a body. Her heartburn in the evening was even worse than the morning sickness had been.

'This will be a bit cold, sorry,' the sonographer apologised as she squirted some gel onto Melissa's tummy.

The little rounded swell had become a source of comfort, a reminder that her baby was growing there. Now, with that changing part of her body exposed to Lachlan's gaze, she felt self-conscious. He'd seen a lot more of her three months ago, but this was different, and she realised she still wanted him to find her attractive. Probably because she couldn't help but be drawn to him, regardless of the chaos they were dealing with in their lives.

He might have been joking about the conversation with his sister earlier, but he *was* handsome, and clearly loyal to his family. There was a big part of Melissa that wished his loyalty included her, that there was more between them so she could have that happy family she always dreamed of. But he was even less of a surety in her life than her parents, or Chris, had been.

She was still attracted to him, there was no doubt, but that only muddied things in her mind. It wasn't easy to separate thoughts of him as a father from the man she'd spent an amazing night with. Otherwise, she wouldn't be so afraid of having him around. The more she liked him, the more he could hurt her. That's why every time they seemed to get closer, she felt the urge to pull away. It was self-preservation. Preparation for the day he left, because experience told her that's what would happen the moment she dropped her guard.

It didn't help when they'd had intimate knowledge of one another. When she could still feel his lips on her, his hands caressing her body…

'Are you okay, Melissa? You look flushed.' Lachlan leaned across the bed to check on her, which only made her hotter round the collar as his warm breath tickled her neck.

'I'm fine. Just excited.' It was true on so many levels. Never more than when he gave her the soppiest smile possible.

'We're just looking to find baby's heartbeat,' the sonographer said. 'It might take a wee while, but don't worry.'

It was easier said than done to follow the medical professional's opinion, when Melissa knew better than anyone how many things could go wrong at this early stage of pregnancy. She felt as though she couldn't breathe until they had proof everything was all right with the baby.

As if sensing her anxiety, or maybe experiencing it too, Lachlan reached for her hand. That simple action of holding her hand in his, feeling the warmth and support in his touch, was enough to help soothe her nerves.

She felt the pressure of the Doppler moving over her belly, searching for signs of life like some sort of rescue mission. Melissa supposed that's what it was in a way, locating her baby's heartbeat to save her life and let her breathe again.

The air was heavy with anticipation, all eyes watching the grainy grey images, ears straining to hear anything which might put their minds at ease.

'There we go.' The sonographer smiled, and suddenly the room echoed with the pulsing sound of their baby's heartbeat.

She squeezed Lachlan's hand. This was real for both of them now. When she glanced up at him, he smiled and dropped a kiss on her head.

'I guess we're really doing this, huh?'

'There's no going back now,' she confirmed, though that niggle at the back of her mind wouldn't let her believe it one hundred percent.

Too many times she'd been let down, left to

pick up the pieces from people who'd promised to be with her forever. Lachlan had never made such a big claim, and that's why thinking he would be here for her when it really mattered would be a mistake. For her sake, and the baby's, she had to keep those defences up a little bit longer.

Lachlan's head was completely taken up with babies these days. Talk about baby brain. He'd been so consumed by thoughts of Melissa and impending parenthood that he'd been unable to sleep after a long shift, and had gone food shopping instead. Only to forget to half the stuff he'd gone in for in favour of buying things for Melissa and the baby.

He knew she'd been struggling with heartburn because he checked in with her daily, either by text or with a call. Although he didn't want to be too full-on, he was aware that she didn't have any other support. He'd asked if she was all right with him keeping up with her, and she'd promised him it was fine. Telling him he had as much right to know what was going on with the baby as she did.

There had been a little tension at the scan, probably due to both of them being anxious. He'd also been afraid she didn't really want him there, but he thought seeing their baby on the screen for the first time together had brought them closer. She'd even let him hold her hand whilst they waited to hear the heartbeat. Progress.

When the baby arrived, he and Melissa would be sharing the childcare, juggling it around their shifts. He was determined to be a present father. Nothing was going to be more important than spending time with his child, and he wanted her to get used to having him around.

No, this wasn't where he'd ever expected to be, but he was committed to being a father, and he was sure he'd grow into the role. He was trying his best.

When he'd seen the baby at the scan, he'd felt a flutter of excitement. It was confirmation he was going to be a father. Thinking about what that would entail gave him more reason to get up in the mornings, and he realised he was looking forward to the prospect of having a child.

He could admit to himself now that part of the problem in his relationship with Julieann after his cancer treatment had been his fear that he'd never be able to be a father. Until he'd got sick, he'd always imagined having a family of his own. It hadn't seemed such an unrealistic prospect then.

However, when it became clear that fathering a baby mightn't be as straightforward as he'd always believed, he'd let fear take over, and it had ended his relationship with Julieann. He'd been afraid to fail her, to have to go through the pain and humiliation of not being able to do something as simple as getting her pregnant. And he'd had enough of hospitals and medical intervention to go through it in order to have a child.

With the decision taken out of his hands, he was allowing himself to get excited about the prospect of watching him or her grow up. Although an unexpected development in his life, this baby was going to be wanted and loved.

'Lachlan? What are you doing here?' Melissa opened her front door, pulling her fluffy pink dressing gown tighter around her.

'Sorry for calling late. I didn't wake you, did I?'

She looked tired and washed out without her make-up. Perhaps it was due to the knowledge she was carrying his child, but Lachlan thought she was even more beautiful now than when they'd first met at the festival.

'I wish. This little one is playing havoc with me.' Melissa rubbed her stomach and yawned.

'I know. That's why I picked up a few pieces for you while I was out shopping. Can I come in?' It was presumptuous of him to turn up on her doorstep at this time of night and expect her to welcome him in, but this pregnancy had awakened a need inside him to protect his family. Like it or not, Melissa was his family now.

He knew it couldn't be any more than that, even though they were having a baby. She'd made it clear she was still grieving the fiancé she'd lost, and he'd been the rebound. They'd been tied together because of a mistake and a lack of common sense. All they could do now was make the most of things and raise this baby as best they could.

The only serious relationship he'd been in had ended badly, and he couldn't afford for that to happen with a baby involved. He didn't want to prioritise his libido over his chance to be a father. If he did start something with Melissa and it didn't work out, it could impact his relationship with his child. Perhaps the only one he'd ever have. He didn't want to let down his son or daughter the way his father had done to him. As much as he liked

Melissa, his relationship with the baby had to come first.

No one could possibly understand how much the absence of a father figure in his life had affected him. Probably because he'd spent his life protecting other people and hiding his true feelings. That responsibility had been heaped onto his shoulders at an early age because of his father, and was the very reason he couldn't afford to forget that the emotional well-being of his child was more important than his own.

'If you've got chocolate in that bag, you're very welcome.' She nodded towards the shopping bag at his feet and opened the door.

'Of course. I told you, I've got your back.' He grinned and followed Melissa into the house, stopping to collect the other gift he'd propped up against the wall.

'I wish you did. It's already hurting, and I've got six months and a few extra pounds to go yet.' Melissa collapsed onto the sofa, obviously feeling sorry for herself.

'You know if I could swap places with you I would.' He didn't want her to be uncomfortable or in pain, though having witnessed Claire in the latter stages of her pregnancy, it appeared to be part of the process.

'I know.' She gave him a half smile, but they both knew she was on her own when it came to dealing with the physical aspect of the pregnancy. Lachlan's role was to support her and make her as comfortable as he could in the meantime.

'Well, I'm hoping I've found something to help you over the next few months.' He showed her the main reason he'd come over.

'What's that?'

'It's a V-shaped pillow. Apparently, they're good for helping your heartburn. They elevate you so you're not sleeping flat. I think it'll help your back too.' He eased her forward and positioned the pillow behind her back.

She shuffled in her chair and leaned back with a contented sigh. 'I'm taking this everywhere with me.'

Lachlan's cheesy grin was directly down to the fact that he'd been able to make her happy and comfortable even for a little while. 'I got you the fleece-lined one so it would be more cosy.'

'You didn't have to, but thank you. I appreciate you coming all this way to bring me a pillow so I can try and get some sleep. Can I get you a cup of tea or anything?' She went to get up, but Lachlan put out a hand to stop her.

'Stay there. I'll make us both a hot drink.' He wanted to make himself useful, to do something for her, because she didn't appear to have anyone else looking after her.

Melissa's parents had apparently taken the news well considering the circumstances, but hadn't mentioned coming back to see her. Lachlan's mum had been over the moon to hear there was going to be a new addition, and thrilled that he was going to be a father. Of course, she'd expressed her wish for him and Melissa to get together and live happily ever after. But he'd made it clear that wasn't on the cards. They had to be realistic.

As far as he could tell, relationships didn't last. His father had walked out on his family, Claire's other half had gone AWOL, and Melissa's parents had effectively abandoned her when she was barely an adult. Lachlan's relationship had ended eventually too. Even Melissa's long-term partner had died, robbing her of their lives together. Nothing could come of imagining that he had a future with her other than co-parenting their child, except heartache. Someone was always left behind, and, given his medical history, he was sure he'd be the one exiting the scene early even if it was against his wishes. Until that time came, he'd do whatever he could for his new little family, even if it required keeping something of an emotional distance. It would be best for both of them long-term. He didn't want to put Melissa through the pain of losing someone she loved again.

Lachlan carried his shopping into the kitchen. Melissa already had her eyes closed, though she had her hand on her chest, heartburn still in attendance. He unpacked the bits and pieces he'd bought to stock her fridge and cupboards, then heated up a cup of milk and added a spoonful of honey.

'Try that. It's supposed to help with the heartburn.'

'What is it?' Melissa inspected the cup as though he was attempting to poison her.

'Hot milk with a spoonful of honey.'

She took the cup and inhaled the smell. 'Mmm. It's so comforting. Reminds me of when I was little. Mum used to heat a little milk in the pan for me every night before bedtime to help me sleep.'

Lachlan was glad that not only had he succeeded in cheering her up, but also that she had some happy childhood memories. Sometimes those could get lost under later traumatic ones. That was partly why he'd worried so much about becoming a father himself. Having witnessed the effect of absentee parents, the toll it took on the children left behind, he didn't want to be responsible for inflicting that trauma on anyone else. Of course, circumstances made that more difficult now, but he would be here for his family as long as possible.

'I hope I haven't overstepped, but I've left some salads and things in the fridge. Apparently, it's better for your heartburn to eat little and often instead of big meals. I brought some bananas and almonds too.'

'You have been doing your homework.'

'Sorry. You're the expert. I'm sure you know all this yourself.' It dawned on him too late that Melissa was more than the mother of his unborn child. She was a qualified midwife who dished out advice to ailing pregnant women every day. He'd got carried away with the idea of providing for her, and had forgotten she was perfectly capable of taking care of herself.

'I'm not very good at taking my own advice, or I wouldn't be in this mess in the first place.' She set down her cup and rubbed her hands over her slight belly.

'I just wanted you to know I'm going to be

here for you both.' After the tension at the scan, he didn't want there to be any doubt about his involvement.

'And we appreciate it.'

In that split second, he imagined the sight of her sitting there with the baby in her arms, whilst he cooked dinner. A cosy domestic scene which, if they'd been in a relationship, wouldn't have been out of order. However, they were still virtual strangers, both with too much baggage to ever provide a stable home life for a child together. He needed to get that thought right out of his head. The baby was his, but its mother wasn't.

'If you've finished your drink, I'll take the cup in and give it a rinse.'

'You don't have to—'

'It's not a problem. You put your feet up.' He'd seen a couple of dirty cups and plates in the sink, so he took the cup into the kitchen and washed them all. At least this way he was doing something useful and still managing to keep a little distance.

Once he'd finished drying and putting away the dishes, he went into the living room to say his goodbyes.

'That's the dishes done. I'm going to head home and let you…sleep.'

Melissa was curled up on the sofa, hugging the pillow like a lover, eyes closed, fast asleep. He doubted it was the conventional way to make use of the present he'd brought, but she was asleep, which was all that mattered. They had a long way to go before they met the rascal causing all the trouble, and she was going to need all the rest she could get between now and then.

She looked serene, a soft smile on her lips that caused him to wonder what she was dreaming about that made her so happy. Probably the baby. Hopefully him too.

He was overcome with a swell of emotion, unfiltered because she was asleep and he was able to drop his defences for a moment. There was no doubt she was beautiful, her red hair spread around her shoulders like wildfire. But since meeting her again, Lachlan realised there was so much more to her. She was strong and independent, and he admired how much she'd achieved on her own. Melissa was an amazing woman and coping tremendously in difficult circumstances. There was no doubt she could manage this pregnancy and parenthood without him, and he counted himself lucky she was allowing him to be part of it.

He brushed a wayward strand of hair from her forehead and bent down to drop a kiss where it had lain. Taking the blanket draped along the back of the sofa, he tucked it around her to keep her warm, and crept out of the room, careful not to wake her. Capturing the picture of her sleeping peacefully with one last lingering look.

The hardest part of all of this was going to be stopping himself from falling for her, because he was pretty sure it had happened the first time he'd kissed her.

Melissa waited until she heard the front door shut before she opened her eyes and sucked in a shaky breath. It had taken all her strength not to pull Lachlan down beside her when he'd kissed her on the forehead. He was being so kind and attentive. It wasn't helping to stymie the attraction she still felt towards him. If anything, it was making it worse. Who wouldn't want a man who brought food, did the dishes, and made sure you had a comfortable pillow? He was certainly making her feel as though she and the baby were important to him. It would be a problem if she got used to it.

Lachlan was trying his best to be a father

to their baby, but that only made her like him more. It was so long since anyone had thought about her feelings or looked after her, it was easy to get swept away in the romance of it. However, the last man she'd fallen for had been cruelly taken from her, and now she had even more to lose with a baby to consider. It was important to protect herself and the baby from being hurt, and not give in to some daydream that they'd be a happy family. She shouldn't throw caution to the wind again simply because Lachlan was an honourable man who didn't shirk his responsibilities.

That meant not turning into a puddle because he'd felt the need to kiss her. Regardless of whether that was a sign that he cared for her in some fashion and hadn't wanted her to know it.

It didn't matter that perhaps her growing feelings towards Lachlan weren't entirely one-sided. They absolutely couldn't act on the impulse that had upended their lives in the first place.

CHAPTER FIVE

'I KNOW IT'S early days in the pregnancy, but I thought it might be nice to get a few ideas for the nursery.' Lachlan opened the door into the store, a world of baby and maternity essentials that Melissa hadn't yet ventured into.

'I am superstitious, so I don't want to buy anything for the baby until closer to my due date, but we can window-shop. I'll probably need to get some maternity clothes anyway. It won't be long until I'm bursting out of everything.' In a short matter of time, her slightly rounded stomach would become the same boulder belly a lot of her patients were carrying, and she'd be needing to pee every few minutes too.

They all displayed similar symptoms around the time of the third trimester. At that 'fed up' stage of pregnancy when everything ached, and any movement was exhausting. When giving birth became just as much about having control of one's body again as meeting the baby. In the end, though, they were all happy simply to have a healthy baby.

'I'm sure you'll still be beautiful.'

Melissa knew he was just pacifying the mother of his unborn child, but a simple compliment from Lachlan still had the ability to make her heart flutter. That was why she'd had to think twice about agreeing to come here with him today. In the end, she'd been forced to face the fact that she would have to make some concessions when he'd been so supportive at the scan. She didn't want to sabotage his relationship with the baby because she was afraid of getting too close to him. If she drove him away permanently, she would be setting her child off in life with the same sense of abandonment and rejection she'd been dealing with. Going on a shopping trip seemed a small price to pay to keep Lachlan happy in the scheme of things.

'Not as beautiful as I know this little one is going to be.' She rested her hands on her belly and put the focus back where it needed to be. On the baby, not her. It was safer that way.

'Well, it's blessed with a double helping of good looks and brains with us as parents. Though I'm not much for interior design, so

I'll leave that up to you. I'll deal with the more practical side of things, like building the cot and painting the walls.'

'Suits me. I'll just supervise from an armchair with a cup of tea in my hand.' They were just joking around, but there was a part of her that was both excited by the prospect of them getting a nursery ready, and terrified that he would be so embedded in her life by that time. It suggested a level of intimacy along with the shared responsibility of parenthood. Everything that she was afraid of.

'As you should. Now, rainbows and unicorns, or trains and cars?' Lachlan held up a pink blanket along with a blue one.

'How about something more neutral?' Melissa countered with lemon teddies.

'Don't you want to know the sex? It would make things so much easier for this kind of thing.'

'I want it to be a surprise. Besides, I don't go in for gender stereotypes.' Melissa sniffed.

'Neither do I as a rule, but I'm desperate to know if I'm going to have a little boy or a girl.' Lachlan's enthusiasm was admirable, but it also set off alarm bells for Melissa.

'Wait, you want to know the sex of our baby?'

'Well, yes.'

'I don't want to plan out a name and a life for my baby before I've even had the chance to meet him or her.'

'Okay. It's not something we have to worry about now. We can discuss it later.' Lachlan dropped the subject and moved on to look at the pushchairs, but the conversation had unnerved Melissa.

They both clearly had different ideas, and though this wasn't a particularly big deal, she was sure they were going to disagree over a lot of decisions. They were sharing the parenting, and that entailed making those big choices together too. Not only now during pregnancy, but those affecting their child its whole life. She was beginning to realise the far-reaching implications of her actions three months ago, but it was too late now. The only way to survive this was to treat it as some sort of business deal, taking out any emotional attachment to Lachlan to safeguard herself and the baby. Not letting herself get too close to him because, like everyone else in her life, the day would come when he would leave her and she'd end up on her own. Dealing with the consequences of letting him get involved in the first place.

'I think I'll go up onto the next floor and try to find a pair of trousers with an elasticated waistband for my ever-expanding stomach.' Melissa excused herself to take the escalator and get a little space.

She'd accepted the invitation to go shopping as a chance to bond as parents over their imminent arrival, but now she was beginning to believe it was a mistake. Lachlan's enthusiasm to be involved was admirable, and would be celebrated if they were any other couple expecting a baby. But it only made her worry more. She didn't want to get drawn into his excitement and forget that they weren't actually together. Once she did that, she could kiss goodbye to what was left of her broken heart. First and foremost, this baby was hers. She'd be the primary carer, and Lachlan had simply been the sperm donor. He might want a relationship with the child, but that's where it had to end. For the sake of her own sanity.

A woman ahead of her was struggling to wrangle the baby on her hip and the youngster holding her hand. The little boy was trying to shake his mother off, and when he succeeded, he charged off up to the top of the escalator.

'Henry! Wait right there!' The harassed mother took off after him, but Little Henry was clearly keen to explore his surroundings, fascinated by the moving walkway. He'd made it to the top of the down escalator, letting his hand drift onto the handrail.

'Henry, that's dangerous. Please stay back.' The mother's tone was getting desperate as she rushed to try and grab him.

Unfortunately, the thrill-seeking Henry had decided to throw his whole body onto the handrail, apparently thinking it was some kind of ride. Melissa tried to make a grab for him as his mother screamed, but he was just out of her reach. She could only watch in horror as the child fell off, hitting the mechanical steps on his way down. He was lying lifeless on the ground floor as his mother's screams echoed around the store.

'Lachlan!' Melissa yelled to draw his attention to the situation. He was a paramedic, able to provide some first aid to the child until they could get him to hospital.

Once Lachlan understood what the commotion was about, he was immediately on his knees beside the boy, trying to rouse him.

'Phone an ambulance,' Melissa directed one of the young cashiers who'd come to see what had happened.

She took the mother's hand and guided her back down the escalator. 'Lachlan's a paramedic. He'll look after Henry.'

Someone brought a chair and a glass of water for the shocked mother, and a first aid kit appeared at Lachlan's request. Melissa went to assist him.

'Is there anything I can do?'

'Unzip his coat for me. He's unresponsive but breathing. There's a head injury and significant bleeding.' Lachlan opened the first aid box while Melissa unzipped the child's jacket and loosened the top buttons of his plaid shirt to try and help him breathe a little better.

'Is Henry going to be okay?' The mother was understandably upset, but the store staff were keeping her at a safe distance from seeing her son and becoming more distressed.

'He's breathing. Hopefully it's nothing serious, but we'll know better when he gets to the hospital. Has someone called an ambulance?' Lachlan was very much in charge of the situation now. Although Melissa had medical know-how, he was the paramedic, used to dealing with such accidents.

'The staff phoned for one. Hopefully it won't take much longer.' Melissa checked

Henry's pulse, relieved to find that it was steady.

Such a serious fall could cause all sorts of problems, from broken bones to spinal cord injuries or brain damage. The best they could hope for was that this was a simple concussion, leaving no lasting damage. Until they got him assessed at the hospital, however, they had to take precautions not to aggravate any injuries.

'I don't think there are any broken bones,' Lachlan said.

That was something, at least, but without X-rays, there was no way of telling if there were any internal injuries.

'Pulse is steady, but there's swelling and bruising around his eye and cheek bone. Can someone get me an ice pack?' Melissa wasn't used to dealing with this kind of medical emergency. Usually there was a baby involved, and she had her bag of medical supplies with her. The one bonus was that she had Lachlan here with her. She was used to working on her own out in the community with the responsibility for the patient entirely on her shoulders. At times like this, she was reminded she didn't have to do everything on her own.

Something she could carry over into her personal life every now and then too. Goodness knew she was going to need the extra support when the baby arrived, and Lachlan would be more than capable of changing a few nappies, or giving a few bottles, if he could single-handedly deal with a medical emergency like this.

Someone handed her a medical ice pack from the first aid kit, and she broke the tube inside to activate it. Holding it against the child's face to try and reduce the swelling, she was struck by how much he looked like his mother. Melissa couldn't help but wonder if their baby would favour her or its father. She was surprised to find she was hoping for a mini-Lachlan. Even though that would mean a constant reminder that she'd gone on to have a family with someone other than Chris, it would be a reminder of Lachlan too.

For some reason, having a part of him in her life was becoming more important than mourning a relationship that, if she was honest, wasn't as wonderful as she liked to remember. Yes, Chris had been her first real love, and she'd thought she'd spend the rest of her life with him, raising their family. But he'd also been a man who hadn't been great at expressing his emotions. Certainly, he'd never shown great enthusiasm when she'd mentioned having children. Lachlan, on the other hand, was here, involved, and ready to be a father.

'You okay, Melissa?' Lachlan was looking at her with concern for her welfare, even during this unforeseen medical drama.

'Yes. Just hoping the ambulance gets here soon.' She offered him a smile to reassure him that she was okay. This wasn't about her, though it was nice to know he was thinking about her, and how treating this small child might be affecting her.

It was difficult enough for all who'd witnessed the accident, including his mother. Though the boy would likely recover, she was sure the majority of those present would never get over the sight of the injury happening. She knew she wouldn't. Her heart was breaking for the mother sobbing nearby. Melissa already felt protective of her growing offspring and knew she'd be devastated if anything happened. Henry was so small and helpless lying here, it was impossible not to be moved.

'Henry? Can you hear me? Can you open your eyes for me?' Lachlan tried repeatedly to get a response to no avail. He cleaned away the blood at the boy's temple until he found the wound causing the problem, and covered it with a sterile dressing.

'He's probably going to need a few stitches, and the hospital will need to do some X-rays to make sure there's no fracture.' He kept the mother informed as he stroked the boy's cheek, trying to rouse him. Showing a sensitivity as well as his professional manner in his actions.

Melissa knew he was going to be a great father.

'Henry? Open your eyes so your mum knows you're okay.'

This time, as Lachlan spoke, the child's eyes began to flutter open.

'Mummy?' he croaked, drawing a sob of relief from his mother.

She dropped to her knees beside her son. 'I'm here, sweetheart. You've had a fall, but you're going to be all right.'

The woman stroked his forehead, ignoring the blood drying in his hair, her love there in every word and gesture.

It proved yet again what a huge undertaking parenting was, being responsible for a young life, emotions tied to the well-being of that tiny human.

Then Melissa thought about Lachlan, how good he was in a crisis, caring and competent. The kind of person she wanted with her to share the responsibility of parenting. Which was just as well when they were inextricably linked for the foreseeable future.

'That was full-on,' Lachlan remarked after Henry, his mother and younger sibling were driven away in the ambulance.

'Yeah. I think seeing a child in danger like that hits harder these days.' Melissa hugged her belly as they made their way back to Lachlan's car.

It was going to make her job even more poignant, bringing lives into the world, once she did it herself. On those rare occasions when a child didn't survive long-term, it was also going to be tougher than ever to deal with. These tiny beings were precious and, though she cherished every one, her own baby was going to be the most important thing in her life.

'I have to admit my heart was in my throat treating him.' Lachlan showed an uncharacteristic display of self-doubt. It hadn't occurred to Melissa that he would feel the same way. He wasn't carrying their baby, but clearly that paternal instinct was kicking in already. This baby was going to change everything for them.

'We've both had a shock.'

'We could probably do with some time to decompress after that. It wasn't the fun shopping experience I imagined when I suggested this outing.' Lachlan got in beside her, buckled his seat belt, and started the short drive home.

'Oh? What were you expecting? A line of shop girls catering to your every whim? Champagne and canapés while you waited?' Melissa couldn't help but tease when deep down she'd known the trip was going to end in disaster. Obviously, she could never have imagined the horrible accident which took place, but nursery shopping with Lachlan would never have been relaxing. Not when she was so torn between wanting him to be an involved father, and worried about getting too emotionally attached to him.

Lachlan glared at her out of the corner of his eye. 'No. I just wanted to spend some time together, making plans for our new arrival.'

His heartfelt reasons for today quietened Melissa's need to tease. She couldn't have asked for a more involved father for her baby, she supposed. It was difficult to work out whether that was a blessing or a curse in the circumstances. The complication was that the more she got to know him, the more she liked him. She was in limbo, with no clear idea of where she was going or what lay ahead. A perpetual state of confusion.

They spent the rest of the short journey in silence, but when they arrived at her house, it didn't seem right to simply send him on his way again.

'Why don't you come in for a cuppa?'

'Are you sure?'

'Yes. It's been a rough morning. Come in.' She got out and closed the car door, not giving him an opportunity to decline. In her experience, it wasn't easy to switch off after a fraught medical event. It seemed pointless for them to be sitting in separate houses, going over every second of what had happened and wondering if they could have done anything differently.

'My turn to make it today. Take a seat,' she called over her shoulder, leaving him to make himself at home. She was glad she'd summoned enough strength to tidy up before she'd left that morning. Thankfully the morning sickness was beginning to ease off, so she was able to function a bit better these days.

When she walked back into the living room, Lachlan was looking at the framed photographs in her bookcase.

'Is this Chris?' he asked, holding up the picture from their engagement. It had become such a part of the furniture, she'd forgotten it was there. Even though Chris had been such a huge part of her life, she wished she had thought to put it out of sight. For both of their sakes—hers and Lachlan's.

Although they weren't together, she didn't want Lachlan to feel uncomfortable being reminded that he wasn't the one she'd wanted a family with. It was also jarring for her to see Chris staring back at her when he hadn't been at the forefront of her mind for some time. She'd been so focused on the baby, and batting away any feelings Lachlan was awakening in her, that she'd forgotten to miss him.

When she'd told her parents that Chris had died, their idea of consoling her had been to say she'd learn to live with her grief. At the time, she'd thought it insensitive to suggest she'd ever get over the loss. She'd even asked them not to come to the funeral. She'd been upset that they thought it would be so easy for her to forget a loved one, the way they seemed to have done when they moved away without her.

Now, however, she could see they'd been right. Life had moved on, and whilst she'd never forget Chris, Lachlan and the baby were actively part of her life. Nothing was going to bring Chris back, and with a child on the way, she couldn't keep living in the past. Everything now was about the future, and unfortunately Chris was no longer a part of that.

'That was taken on our engagement day. We had a five-year plan of what we wanted to accomplish before we got married. As it turned out, we waited too long.' Whilst she would probably never get over losing him, or the unfairness of being denied their life together, Lachlan had helped her move into a new chapter of her life. Albeit unwittingly.

The pregnancy had been an accident, but ultimately she thought it was the best thing to happen to her. It had given her someone else to love, a future she hadn't wanted to look forward to until now. This baby had given her life meaning again.

'I'm sorry. And that was your last relationship before we...you know.' Lachlan turned a very becoming shade of red as he referenced their liaison at the festival. It was kind of cute that he was so coy about it. He certainly hadn't been shy at the time.

Melissa nodded. 'And you?'

Lachlan nodded too, the redness glowing brighter. He set the photo back and took the cup of tea offered before coming to sit on the sofa. 'I'd split with my ex about six months before that.'

'I'm sorry.' That would explain why he hadn't wanted to get into anything serious.

'Melissa, there's something I haven't told you…'

Although she had no way of knowing what was coming next, all the blood from Melissa's head seemed to drain down into her toes, leaving her light-headed. Whatever it was, it wasn't good. Despite all of the preventative measures she'd tried to take, if he told her now that he was backing off, she knew she'd be devastated. She'd got used to having him around, even if her growing feelings for him had made her uncomfortable at times.

'What is it?' She swallowed hard, bracing herself for what he had to say.

'Before we met… I underwent treatment for testicular cancer.'

'Oh.' It was a bigger shock to her system

than the news she'd been expecting, and no less concerning. Not only for Lachlan, but because of what it meant for her and the baby too.

Although it seemed selfish to concern herself with thoughts of what would happen to them if they lost him now that she'd let him be part of their lives, she had more reason than ever to be afraid of the consequences. What if the same thing happened to him that had happened to Chris?

'I had a testicle removed. Went through chemotherapy and a surgical reconstruction. I know I should have told you sooner, but it's not something I casually drop into conversation. It was a difficult time, and when we met at the festival, I was celebrating the end of my treatment. I hadn't expected that we'd see each other again, and it didn't seem like something you needed to worry about. But since you've been honest with me...'

'I appreciate you telling me.' There was no logical reason for her to feel angry that he'd kept this information from her until now, but she couldn't help it. Whilst she was glad he'd come through it, and sorry that he'd had to deal with such a serious medical issue, she wished he'd told her sooner.

If she'd known he had serious medical issues, she would have been even more careful about getting too close. Melissa had every sympathy for Lachlan, but she'd already been through too much to face the potential of another loss in her life.

'I don't want any secrets. I know we're not a couple, but we are going to be in each other's lives for a long time. I hope.' Lachlan smiled, but his dark humour only served to make Melissa more concerned about what the future held.

It was a stark reminder that nothing was guaranteed, and she suddenly realised she didn't want to think of a life without him in it.

She could understand now what had drawn them together at the music festival, both having gone through a difficult time and looking for a new start. He was likely to have been carrying serious emotional wounds, especially if his partner had dumped him for something beyond his control. It seemed callous in the circumstances. Even if Melissa had known about Chris's illness, she would've wanted to spend every second possible with him. She wouldn't have abandoned him when he needed her most. Too bad she hadn't been given the chance to prove that.

Lachlan made a face. 'In a way…facing my own mortality like that made me think about what I really wanted in life. She was keen to start a family, and I decided I wasn't.'

The words were like a punch to Melissa's gut. As she had worried all along, Lachlan never wanted any of this. He was only here out of a sense of duty, and that did not seem the basis of a long-term relationship with his child. If his intention had been to remain foot-loose and fancy-free, he'd probably planned to travel and have fun. Now he was tied down to a baby. What if someone, or something, more exciting came along that he felt he couldn't resist? Or, worst-case scenario, he got sick again? Either way, there was no guarantee Lachlan would be here for the long haul. Another reason not to get used to having him around, saving the day.

'It's ironic, I know, given the circumstances. But what's done is done. We have to make the most of the situation now.' Definitely not the words of a man who seemed as ecstatic about the prospect of becoming a father as she'd thought. Melissa wondered if his apparent interest so far had been for her benefit. An attempt to make her think this was what he wanted so she didn't feel bad. He was a people-pleaser, but she wanted someone who would be honest with her about his feelings so there would be no unpleasant surprises down the line. She didn't think she could take any more.

'If your heart isn't in this, Lachlan, now's the time to back out. I don't want you disappearing when this baby is old enough to understand rejection. I can manage on my own.' She set down her tea, prepared to go into battle until she got to the truth. It was better to bring things to a head now, before the baby was born, so they all knew where they stood.

It felt as though he had as little interest in a family as Chris. Except they'd been left no choice in the matter. Lachlan hadn't been given the space to put off parenthood until he thought he was ready. He was going to be a father, and now she was more worried than ever that Lachlan would have second thoughts at some point between now and the baby's arrival.

He was frowning at her. She much preferred him smiling, but this needed to be said. There was no point in pretending he was on board if he was going to bail out when reality hit home.

'I thought we'd been through this, Melissa? I went to the scan, took you shopping today, because I'm a part of this. No, it wasn't where I thought life was going to take me, but I am one hundred percent committed.'

'You were so against starting a family that you ended your relationship. How can you change your mind over something so life-altering for a woman you barely know?'

He set his tea down on the coffee table and sank back into the chair, taking his time with how he answered. Melissa didn't know whether she should be pleased he was considering his reply so deeply, or worried he was about to let her down and thinking of a way to do it gently.

'I grew up without a father. My mum worked day and night to pay the bills, and as the eldest child, I had to step up. I took on responsibility for my brother and sister when I was little more than a child myself. I didn't want to carry on that legacy into another family.'

Melissa could understand that way of thinking. It would have been easy for her to do the same, forgo a family of her own so she didn't end up disappointing them the way her parents had. They simply chose different ways of dealing with their pasts and protecting their hearts. Now their mistake had disrupted all of their carefully laid plans.

'I was the opposite. When Mum and Dad moved abroad and left me behind, I was desperate to fill that void. I couldn't wait to have a family, but Chris wanted to hold off until we had our careers set and money in the bank.' Thinking about it now, he hadn't been as keen about starting a family, always finding excuses—they didn't have enough in savings, he wanted that promotion first, it was best to wait until after they got married so they wouldn't upset anyone. In the end, they'd agreed on their five-year plan, but she suspected that was only to stop her going on about it in the meantime.

Perhaps she had been trying to overcompensate for the void her parents had left in her life, but she'd thought Chris had wanted the same things she did. That could be why she kept doubting Lachlan's words, worried he was only saying things to keep her happy and didn't actually mean any of them.

'It wasn't a bad plan. Neither of you knew what was coming.'

'Hmm. I think he was just trying to put it off. In hindsight, I was the only one talking about a family in our future. I think I was projecting my issues onto our relationship.'

'I think we're all guilty of that. I let my feelings for my father destroy what I had with my ex.'

'Why were you so convinced you were going to stuff things up too? That you weren't going to be around?' Melissa wanted to know why he was so afraid of being a father himself, in case it came back to haunt both of them in the future.

Lachlan cleared his throat. 'The cancer. There's always a chance it will come back. I didn't want to have the thought hanging over my family that someday I wasn't going to be there. That I would be responsible for another child growing up without a father.'

Melissa swallowed down the sudden surge of bile rising inside her. Circumstances hadn't allowed them to factor that into any decision to start a family. She was just getting used to his support, and now he was reminding her that he might not be around forever. Everything she'd been afraid of from the moment she'd told him he was the father. It might have seemed selfish when Lachlan was the one who was dealing with health problems, but she'd already lost Chris, and she couldn't imagine going through it again. Didn't want to.

'But you're okay now? You got the all-clear?' Melissa tried to keep the rising hysteria from her voice, worried there was something wrong that he hadn't told her about.

'Yes. I suppose I'm just being paranoid.' His smile went some way to reassure her, but her stomach was still twisted into knots.

'It's understandable, but how does it make you feel knowing you *are* going to be a father now? That the decision has been taken out of your hands?' Melissa understood he had good reason to be wary of getting involved, given his own personal history, and not knowing what the future held for him. However, she didn't want him to end up resenting her or the baby, blaming them for trapping him in a situation he never wanted.

'Perhaps it's for the best things worked out this way. It's forced me to realise not every-thing is in my control. The truth is, I had wanted a family once. Before the cancer. But afterwards, I wasn't sure I could even have children. I told myself I didn't want a family, but I think I'd convinced myself of that because I couldn't spend the rest of my life trying and being left disappointed. Or worse, what if I did have children and ended up leaving them the way my father left us? It's my fault the relationship ended, because I was afraid. I might have beaten the cancer once, but that doesn't mean it won't get me in the end.' His wobbly smile was heartbreaking. Lachlan had been so strong for Melissa and the baby, and the whole time he'd clearly been worrying that the cancer would return. He'd been under tremendous strain, yet supporting them both when they'd needed it. Who'd been there for him?

'It doesn't mean it will either. I imagine we're both terrified about what's going to happen, but as long as we know we're in it together, I think we'll be okay.' She told herself his fear was not her reality. Mainly because it was her fear, too, that he'd be taken away, leaving her on her own with the baby.

'I'm here for as long as I have breath in my body. You both mean too much for me to go anywhere.' Lachlan leaned forward as he spoke, gazing so intensely at her, Melissa couldn't breathe.

She wanted to believe everything he said. Not only that he didn't intend on going anywhere anytime soon, but that she meant more to him than someone he was simply stuck with. Because, despite all the reasons she shouldn't, Melissa knew she was falling deeper for him every day. The way he was looking at her now made her think that everything was going to work out, and she might even get that happy family she'd always wanted. It was heady, and, when he leaned in closer, his eyes trained on her mouth, irresistible.

Lachlan knew he shouldn't, hadn't realised he was going to, but he was definitely about to kiss Melissa. He'd been wanting to from the second he'd laid eyes on her again, their time at the festival burned in his memory, and on every part of his body. As her eyes fluttered shut and she tilted her face up to meet him, he realised she wanted this too. That's when the last thread of his common sense snapped.

He sought her lips with his, the soft sweetness he knew he'd find there, and it was everything he remembered. Melissa relaxed into the kiss, and it only made him crave more. He cupped her face in his hands and deepened the kiss, gently coaxing her tongue with his. When his lips were meshed with hers, his mind full of thoughts of how she was making him feel, everything else melted away.

He wasn't thinking about the accident at the store, or his uncertain future. Not even worrying about what kind of father he was going to be. All he could think about was Melissa and how much he wanted to be with her.

Learning more about her background, how she'd lost her fiancé, only made him admire her more. Her strength and resilience were immeasurable, but he didn't want to let her down. Along with his sister, she was one of the most important things in his life right now.

When he'd moved to the city, he'd been prepared to face new challenges. Though he thought he would be living a life free from responsibilities. He never expected he'd have to step in to support his sister, or that he'd have to get used to the idea of becoming a father himself. The good part of all of this was that he'd got to see Melissa again. She was going to be a permanent fixture in his life from now on, and he didn't want to do anything to ruin that.

Kissing her when she was clearly still grieving for her fiancé probably wasn't the best way to keep her on side. She was vulnerable, especially after what they'd witnessed today. He'd be the worst kind of person to take advantage of her now.

Lachlan reluctantly pulled away, her dazed expression and kiss-swollen lips making him regret his decision already.

'Lachlan?' She blinked at him with big bush-baby eyes, which only served to make her look more vulnerable.

'Sorry. I shouldn't have done that. It's been a difficult day for both of us.' He scrabbled back in his seat, desperate to put some distance between them.

'It's not the first time we've kissed, Lachlan.' Melissa's hands went to her belly, reminding him they'd done a lot more than that in the past. But there was more to lose now.

He got to his feet. 'I know, but I think we should just put this behind us, like the festival, and carry on as we were. Focus on being good parents for the baby.'

Melissa nodded soundlessly, leaving him to ramble to cover the silence. She regretted having given in to temptation. 'If you need anything, just give me a ring, and let me know when your next appointment is so I can support you. Don't get up. I'll let myself out.'

Lachlan practically stumbled out the door in his desperation to get away from his latest faux pas. If he didn't reel in his attraction to Melissa, he was going to ruin everything. All being well, there were six months of this pregnancy left, and he needed to back off from any romantic notions he might have towards her. He'd lied when he referred to the festival, pretending that he'd ever been able to put that behind him. That was the very reason he couldn't keep on kissing her and saying it didn't mean anything. It would end in heartbreak somewhere down the line.

From now on, he'd have to try and limit his interactions with Melissa to public places, and preferably only regarding the baby. It was the only way to protect himself and ensure this baby had two parents present when he or she arrived. He didn't want to give Melissa any reason to give him the heave ho. If he hadn't done so already...

This wasn't a casual relationship between two strangers that could be set aside so they could go on with normal life. They were physically and emotionally tied to one another through the baby they'd conceived. A kiss was much more than a kiss now, and a failed romance could push him out of his child's life before it was even born. There was too much at stake to risk it on an attraction he couldn't be sure would last. He wasn't going to be another absentee father.

CHAPTER SIX

'I CAN'T BELIEVE you're back with your baby daddy and you didn't tell me until now.' Lydia had reacted just the way Melissa knew she would. Loudly. That's why she'd waited until they were outside of the workplace to tell her that Lachlan was back on the scene.

In hindsight, the end of a busy shift hadn't been the ideal time, when she was too tired to deal with her friend's resulting histrionics. Also, Lydia was driving home, her phone apparently on speaker, and Melissa didn't want her to crash the car in the process. However, given that Lachlan seemed a little more distant since that kiss, she thought she could do with the extra support.

He was still showing up for her when needed, but there was something missing between them. As though he was deliberately keeping her at arm's length. She was worried that he was gearing up to walk away, the kiss crossing a line he didn't think they could ever recover from. He was equally to blame for letting it happen, and she didn't see why she should be punished for it. Her hormones were all over the place as it was without him kissing her whenever the mood took him, and walking away when it didn't.

Melissa was aware the day in the store had been challenging, and, when they'd opened up to one another about their pasts, emotional. She didn't know if that was why he'd kissed her, because they'd shared deeply personal information. Neither did she know what had sent him scurrying from the house like a scalded cat other than regret, but she wasn't going to chase him. She'd told him from the start it was his decision whether or not to be in their child's life, and she wasn't going to force him to be in hers either. Not least because she didn't want him to think she was desperate for something more in their relationship. Regardless of how much she was missing the connection she'd had with him. These days he felt more like a stranger than ever. It was telling that she was already roping Lydia in as a replacement for the void he'd left in her life after such a short time.

'I wish you wouldn't call him that. His

name's Lachlan.' It wasn't as though she'd had a string of lovers and narrowed it down to the one who'd actually fathered her baby. She knew exactly who she'd gone to bed with and when the baby had been conceived.

'So, where is he? When do I get to meet him?'

'One step at a time. I don't want to scare him off. We're still getting used to the idea of parenting together, and if things don't work out, I want to know that you'll be there if I need you.' She didn't want to use her friend, but having Lachlan in her life had made her realise she didn't have to do everything on her own. Lydia had offered her support, and Melissa had to get used to accepting help. When the baby came, she might need it.

'Of course. Auntie Lyds is on standby. I do hope things work out for you two though. You deserve some happiness.'

'I don't think it's on the cards for us, but as long as he's a good dad to the baby, I'll be happy.'

Lachlan had told her time and time again he would be here for her and the baby as long as he had breath in his body. It seemed selfish, and unrealistic, for her to want more now.

Melissa hung up and decided to take her

weary body to bed. She'd just reached the top of the stairs when she realised she'd left her phone in the living room. The thought crossed her mind to leave it there, but she needed her alarm to get up for work in the morning. With a resigned groan, she turned around and began to make the descent. Unfortunately, she somehow missed the next step, her foot slipping off the edge and causing her to lose her balance. Before she knew it, she was mid-air, falling down the rest of the stairs, her head and back bumping hard against the steps until she lay in a heap on the ground.

It took her a moment to gather her thoughts, to process what had happened. Then her hands went instinctively towards her bump. She'd had a very hard fall, and though it was still early days in the pregnancy, it was possible that the baby had been hurt. Before she started to panic, she told herself her body was designed to protect the baby, as was the amniotic sac, but then her mind started to race. A placental abruption could occur in the event of a blunt trauma and restrict the baby's oxygen supply, or cause internal bleeding for the mother. Although she didn't think she'd hit her abdomen directly, she didn't want to take any chances. She'd never forgive herself if she didn't get checked out and something happened to the baby.

Unfortunately, she didn't have her phone at hand to contact anyone. Though she was afraid to move, she knew she had to. Melissa slowly got to her feet, bracing a hand against the wall, only for an excruciating pain to shoot up through her leg and collapse her again. She'd obviously injured her ankle if she wasn't able to put any weight on it without it giving way beneath her.

After a few more attempts to stand, and some swearing, she managed to drag herself into the living room. As she crumpled into an armchair, she was sobbing, both from the pain and fear. She grabbed her phone to call Lachlan, the only person she wanted here with her. He would hold her hand, talk to her in that soothing way he spoke to patients, and generally reassure her that everything was going to be okay.

She brought up her contact list, desperate to reach out to him, knowing he'd be at her door in minutes if he thought something was wrong. But she knew he'd only come because he felt a responsibility towards her, and that wasn't why she wanted him to be with her.

She needed more than he was apparently willing to give. Reluctantly, and with fear threatening to block her airways, she dialled 999.

'Hello. I need an ambulance please,' she said when prompted, holding her belly with one hand and praying her baby would make it.

Despite starting this pregnancy journey with a great deal of trepidation, her baby was the only good thing in her life right now. The only family she had here, and the only one she had a future with. To have it all taken away from her now would be devastating. This baby meant everything to her, and she was so looking forward to meeting him or her.

'Hang in there, jelly bean,' she whispered, hoping for once in her life, if she loved someone enough, they would stay with her.

'Pregnant woman has taken a tumble down the stairs. We should go and check her over.' Scot, the ambulance driver, relayed the basics of the call to Lachlan.

'Put your foot down, mate. I don't want to hang about on this one.' It hit hard, as everything mother- and baby-related did these days. Melissa was constantly on his mind. He wondered if she was okay and marvelled at how he'd managed to cock things up so badly by kissing her.

Perhaps he'd got so wrapped up in the idea of having Melissa and the baby permanently in his life that he'd forgotten all the reasons why he shouldn't give in to that attraction. His focus had to be on his relationship with his baby, not its mother. By kissing her, trying to take their involvement beyond simply being parents, he ran the risk of losing both of them. The last thing he wanted when everything he did was to try and be a present father to their baby.

To right his mistake in crossing that line, he'd had to back off, and make do with the odd text to see how she was. The next few months attending prenatal appointments and not being physically near her would be difficult, but a sacrifice he'd have to make to be the best father he could be.

Scot typed the address into the satnav, and Lachlan's insides seemed to plummet into his shoes.

'What was the name?'

'Moran. Melissa Moran.'

'I don't care how you do it, but get us there at warp speed.'

'You know her?'

'She's the mother of my unborn child, Scot.' Lachlan knew it was news to his colleague that he'd even been seeing anyone, never mind that they were expecting a baby, but nothing was more important than Melissa and the baby. If he'd thought he wasn't up to fatherhood, the panic, the complete fear that his child was in danger gripping his heart, was proof that he was a parent already.

Suddenly, it seemed as though the lights, sirens, and Scot's expert driving couldn't get them to Melissa's place fast enough.

'Sorry, mate. I didn't know. I'm sure they'll both be okay.' Scot did his best to reassure him, but Melissa was only just in her second trimester, and wasn't completely out of danger of miscarrying. Besides, they didn't know how serious the fall had been. Though she would've been concerned about the baby, he was sure she would've downplayed her own injuries. He couldn't bear to see either of them hurt.

'Let's hope so.' Lachlan grabbed his kit and jumped out of the ambulance the second they pulled up outside the house.

'She keeps a spare key under the flower pot.' He'd rolled his eyes when he'd heard that one. It wasn't exactly security-conscious, but she thought he should know in case of emergencies. Just like this one. Now he was grateful for her presence of mind.

'Melissa? It's Lachlan. You called for an ambulance?' he yelled into the house as soon as he unlocked the door. A desperate need to know for himself that she and the baby were all right spurred him on.

'Lachlan? I'm in here.'

He hated the sound of her sobbing and how small her voice seemed from the living room. It told of her fragility, of how frightened she'd been here all on her own, when he should've been with her. He'd been so caught up in his own fears and doing the right thing by the baby that he'd neglected to think of her and how she might need him.

Lachlan rushed in to find her curled up in a chair, her arms wrapped protectively around her bump. His throat was suddenly clogged with a lump of emotion at the sight of her so vulnerable and afraid. Despite everything he'd been trying to avoid recently, he had to reach out and hug her tight. She looked as though she really needed it.

'It's going to be okay.'

He felt her nod against his chest, heard her soft sob as her tears soaked through his clothes. Although he'd been fighting it for so long, there was no more denying he cared deeply for this woman. He would've done anything to make things okay for her. He held her like that for a moment, as much for his sake as hers, then let go to check her over.

Thankfully all of Melissa's vital signs were normal. Her heart rate was a little elevated, but that was to be expected in the circumstances.

'I checked the baby's heartbeat with my own Doppler,' she offered.

'Of course you did,' Lachlan said with a smile. Her first thought would always be for the baby, and he was relieved that both of them appeared relatively uninjured by the fall. Though he would still worry until they'd had the official all-clear at the hospital.

'We'll take you in anyway, and maybe get an ultrasound to put both of our minds at rest.'

Melissa nodded, offering no resistance as he helped her out of the chair, though he did notice her wince as she got to her feet. 'I think I hurt my ankle on the way down.'

'Why didn't you say? Scot, can you get the wheelchair, please?' He made her sit down again to rest up until it was in situ, wishing she'd stop being so damned independent.

Yes, he'd been guilty of holding back, of bottling up his feelings. But the thought of losing her had made him see just how damned important she was to him. He wanted to take care of her.

If they were to get back to the sort of camaraderie they'd had before he'd kissed her and complicated things all over again, they'd have to forget it had ever happened. The only important thing was that she and the baby were all right.

He and Melissa had a lot to sort out before their baby made an appearance. Important things like childcare and what financial contribution he'd be making. Hopefully he'd get over this crush at some stage so he could function as a present father, instead of a mooning teenage boy who couldn't keep his feelings in check.

Lachlan was as relieved as Melissa to see their baby on the screen, apparently unharmed by her tumble down the stairs. In fact, he got such a thrill out of watching the little heartbeat that he'd be permanently tuned in to that channel given half a chance. It was a constant reminder that his body hadn't failed him after all. That he was going to be a dad.

Only once Melissa was sure the baby was okay did she consent to getting checked over herself. She'd insisted on going to X-ray on her own, and he'd had to resist trailing after her.

When he finally saw her bustling through the corridor, he felt as though he could breathe again. She had that effect on him. Whenever she was around, his life just seemed so much better. That's why these past days had been so hard, not being around her.

'As suspected, just a sprain.' She showed off the bandage wrapped around her ankle.

'Don't scare me like that again.' Lachlan stood up from his chair and hugged her, wanting to cling onto her, and have that tangible reassurance that she was okay. He was forced to let go so she could sit down, before things got weird.

The thought of what could have happened was too devastating to imagine.

This woman carrying his baby was the most important person in the world to him. And he'd been doing his best to keep her at arm's length. Suddenly his logic seemed skewed. Instead of worrying about a cancer that might not return, or being as unreliable as his father, he should have been concentrating on the present. On the good things he did have in his life.

Melissa rubbed his back in that comforting way that reminded him he wasn't alone. Her touch was the contact he'd been longing for, not just tonight, but from the second he'd left her house the night they'd kissed.

'I'm sorry I haven't been around.'

'It doesn't matter.' The smile she gave him was too bright to be believable. He had hurt her by disappearing.

'I should have been there for you tonight.'

'It's all right. It would've been a little weird if you'd been standing at the bottom of my stairs all night, waiting for me to fall. No harm done.'

Despite her reassurance, Lachlan wanted to make it up to her in some way, and to keep an eye on her. 'Have you had anything to eat tonight?'

'I was too tired after my shift to cook.'

'Why don't I go home with you and make sure everything's all right? Maybe we could make something to eat.'

'I told you, it's not necessary.'

'I don't want to be alone,' he finally said. If he went home, he knew he'd focus on the events of the night and worry about what might have happened. As well as wondering all night if she was really okay. Plus, he wanted to be there if she needed him.

'Okay then, you can come home with me and spend the night.'

Lachlan cocked an eyebrow at the invitation, drawing a sigh from Melissa.

'Don't worry, it's only so I can make sure you don't give yourself an injury beating yourself up. You'll be on the sofa, mister.'

She made him smile for the first time that night. Her assessment was spot-on. She clearly knew him well already.

Lachlan took her outstretched hand and let her lead him away. He couldn't think of anything better than spending the night with Melissa. In any capacity.

CHAPTER SEVEN

'Do you want to help me in the kitchen?' Melissa was worn out by the night's events, but she knew she wouldn't sleep.

Not with the added stress of Lachlan being in her house to keep her awake. She wasn't hungry either, but she had her baby to look after. Besides, making something to eat would give them a focus away from their personal issues.

He'd surprised her that night at the house when he'd kissed her. Though he'd been caring and considerate towards her, up until then she hadn't sensed that he might have had any feelings for her other than the need to take care of the mother of his baby. That kiss had said otherwise. It hadn't been a platonic peck on the lips, but a display of want which seemed to have been bubbling away for some time. She knew, not only because she'd been on the receiving end, but because she'd felt the same way. The feelings she'd been trying so hard to keep a lid on had suddenly burst forth, resulting in that spontaneous passion which seemed to take them both by surprise.

Tonight he'd shown the tenderness he obviously felt towards her along with that attraction. Lachlan had done his best to reassure her things would be okay, and at the same time had been concerned for her well-being. This felt like more than basic lust, or a situation they'd been forced into. Melissa could see he actually cared about her. Something that was irresistible to a girl who'd been abandoned, and she was weary of fighting against every instinct making her want to revel in it.

'Sure.' He took his jacket off, hung it in the hall, and followed her into the kitchen.

They both needed the distraction after everything they'd been through together that night. The fear and uncertainty they'd both expressed waiting to find out if their baby was all right had brought them closer than ever. Though she knew it was probably a bad idea to bring him here in those circumstances, having him with her was all she wanted. In the end, her heart had won out over her head.

'I thought I could just make us some soup.

Proper comfort food, and it'll warm us up. Is that okay?'

'Yeah. I don't think I could face a big meal.'

'Good. Well, if you're not going to sit down and take it easy, maybe you could chop the vegetables, and I'll rinse the lentils.' It would be filling and comforting, as well as nutritious. Just what they needed right now.

Melissa made up some vegetable stock and found some bacon in the fridge, so she chopped and cooked that to add to the onions, celery, and carrots Lachlan had cut.

'You're pretty nifty with a knife,' she said.

'Years of practice feeding everyone. Mum was always working, so it fell to me to make dinner most nights. I can get very creative on a food budget too.' The ghost of a smile teased his lips as he seemed to conjure the memories. Though Melissa was sure it must've been a struggle for him.

'That can't have been easy for you.' Despite her estrangement from her parents now, they'd been there for her when she was young. She hadn't had to worry about grown-up things like finances and feeding a family.

Her parents had been traditional; mum had been at home taking care of her and the housework, while Dad went to work to support them. That was why it had hurt so much when they'd moved abroad without her. They hadn't seemed to consider how lost and abandoned she would feel without them. Melissa supposed she'd taken them for granted, and perhaps she'd let her anger get in the way of maintaining a relationship with them.

In a perfect world, she would've had them here with her, but that wouldn't have been fair to them. She only wished she'd realised this sooner. Then she might have more support when their grandchild arrived. Hopefully she still had some time to make amends and find some way to have them back in her life, and her baby's.

'No. Dad leaving made me grow up pretty quickly. I felt responsibility for everyone in his absence, and I didn't want to let anyone down. Looking back, the burden shouldn't have fallen to me, and I do resent my father for leaving us like that. I think that's why the thought of becoming a dad myself was something that terrified me at times. I want to be part of my child's life, and the prospect of the cancer returning casts a shadow over that. I hate the thought that I won't be here for our baby someday, and that he or she might resent me for that.'

'I hope it never comes to that.' Even the idea of it sent shivers up and down her spine. She'd tried not to focus on his illness and what it could mean for the future. It was out of her control, but it was probably also why she'd been holding back her feelings for him. Afraid that even if he did want to be part of her life, that fate would steal him away from her just like Chris.

Except none of that was Lachlan's fault. It didn't seem fair to lay the blame at his feet for something he was powerless to prevent. Just like his father walking out. Not being honest about how much she cared for him seemed like a punishment neither of them deserved. Perhaps an even worse fate than if she gave in to those feelings and things didn't work out.

'Me too.'

'Do you see much of the rest of your family?'

'Probably not enough. That was my brother Duncan I was with at the festival. He's married with children, so we usually only see each other at special occasions. And Mum still works a lot. I think she's going to come and stay with Claire when the baby arrives, and I'm hoping we can convince her to move permanently. It will be nice to have her here when our little one arrives too.' Lachlan was clearly a family man who, despite his talk about starting a new life, wanted to gather all of his loved ones around him again.

Melissa still wasn't sure if that included her or not. She envied that close familial bond. On nights like this, she missed having her own family around her. Perhaps having Lachlan stay here tonight was as much for her benefit as it was his.

'I might try reaching out to my parents again. I haven't seen them in so long, and I might need them...' She didn't know if they would be willing to come back specially for her and the baby, but she wanted to open those channels of communication again at least. Maybe motherhood had made her grow up.

'I can understand why you'd want them around, but you know I'll be here for you regardless.' He held her gaze, conveying the sincerity of his commitment to her with one blue-eyed look. It was all she needed to be swept off her feet.

For a moment, that chemistry was back between them, simmering away like the lentil soup on the stove. Thankfully it bubbled over before she and Lachlan did.

'I'll get this. You pull out some dishes and

butter some bread for us.' He took control of both situations, moving the saucepan off the heat and shutting down any notion of another kiss at the same time. Even though his gaze had lingered on her mouth a little too long to be considered disinterested.

On this occasion, Melissa let him boss her around in her own home because his actions were safer than the ideas her mind had conjured up. It didn't matter that getting personally involved now would lead to all sorts of complications. Today had been emotional and frightening for them both, and it wasn't over yet. Clinging to Lachlan was the easy way out, but she'd have to get used to dealing with the emotional stuff on her own if he didn't want that kind of relationship with her. Though his actions tonight said that he was involved as more than a victim of circumstance. She could tell he cared about her as much as the baby. Whether either of them wanted to act on that, and complicate things even further between them, was another matter. Next time she was in trouble, he mightn't be there for her, and it wouldn't do to think otherwise.

They sat down at the kitchen table, giving their late-night, post trauma dinner some sense of normality.

'This is so good,' Lachlan said after taking his first spoonful.

'Just what we needed.' The warmth filling her empty belly was a poor substitute for Lachlan's kisses, but it was tasty and comforting.

'There's still plenty left. Is it okay if I take some with me tomorrow?'

'Of course. I have some containers you can use.'

He yawned as he took his dishes over to the sink to wash up. He put her to shame—she'd happily have left the dishes until tomorrow. She supposed his attitude towards domestic chores was another throwback to his childhood, when he'd been expected to keep house in his mother's absence. It was a lot to put on a young boy's shoulders, and no wonder that he seemed to place everyone else's needs before his own. The difficult thing for her to figure out was whether his actions towards her and the baby were in the same vein. Was it out of responsibility he felt, rather than wanting to be there for them?

If it was the former, it mightn't prove sufficient for him to stick around long-term, despite his assertions. Someday he might feel a stronger responsibility towards someone else and follow it instead.

'You must be exhausted. I'll go and get some bedding and make up the sofa for you.' She left him to get settled and shuffled off to raid the cupboards for extra pillows and blankets. It wasn't often that she had anyone sleeping over. Only Lydia if she'd had one too many on a night out and crashed here. When she wouldn't have cared if it was a sofa or a doorway she was sleeping in.

When she returned to the living room, arms laden with bedding, she almost dropped the heap. Lachlan was sitting on her sofa, bare-foot, bare-chested, naked apart from his boxer shorts. It took her a moment to regain her composure and wipe away her drool.

Was it her imagination, or had he got hotter in the three months since she'd last seen him naked? Perhaps it was because he was more than a stranger now. Or that he was the kind of man who looked after pregnant women and did the dishes. Most likely it was down to the sight of the patch of dark hair on his chest, and the taut abdominal muscles she could have played noughts and crosses on. The last time he'd shown this much flesh, she'd been too engrossed in what they'd been doing to pay close attention. She was making up for it now. It was all she could do not to go and make herself some popcorn to better enjoy the show.

'Sorry. I was just making myself comfortable,' he said, grabbing a cushion and clutching it to his chest. Probably to stop her ogling him.

It jolted her back out of her daydream.

'Of course. No problem. I guess I'm just not used to having half-naked men laying about my house.' She tried to make a joke out of it, but averted her eyes as she set about making a bed for him on the sofa.

He stood up to move out of her way, and she congratulated herself for managing not to stare at his backside. Hormones, she told herself.

'Thanks again for letting me stay here. I just want to be close. To be here for you and the baby in case you need me. At least for tonight.' His words might have been more comforting if he hadn't put a time limit on his need to be near her.

'It's not necessary, but thank you.'

'It's great living on your own until something like this happens and you realise you need people around you.'

'I can't say living on my own is all that great, but I suppose the house will be full again soon enough.' That would be the biggest blessing of all of this. She would never be on her own again. In a few months, the house would be full of baby things and a precious little one to give her the family she'd been missing. Then she could focus on what she had in her life, instead of what she'd lost.

'Sorry. I didn't mean to bring up any bad memories for you—'

'Night, Lachlan.'

She left him to get sorted for the night, not wanting to talk about losing Chris. Because she hadn't thought about him until just now.

Surprisingly, Melissa managed to fall asleep once her head hit the pillow. The events of the evening had apparently taken their toll. However, she was woken at all hours of the morning by that familiar burning sensation in her chest. Heartburn was the curse of her pregnancy, and very little seemed to ease it. Now she had the added pain of a sprained ankle to increase her discomfort.

She lay on for some time, trying to force

herself back to sleep, but her body refused to cooperate. In the end she had no other choice but to creep downstairs on her injured ankle in search of some relief.

Not wanting to turn the light on and disturb Lachlan, she felt her way along in the dark until she reached the kitchen. She opened the fridge just a fraction to keep the light to a minimum, and reached in for the milk.

'You couldn't sleep either?'

The voice coming from the shadows made her jump, and she dropped the milk onto the kitchen floor. The contents spilled out.

Once she realised it was only Lachlan, she pulled herself together again and turned on the light. He was sitting at the breakfast bar in his boxers, blinking at the bright light.

'Sorry. I didn't mean to scare you.'

'I thought you were asleep.' She bent down to pick up the container and stop any more milk leaking out, though the floor was already covered in the stuff.

'I tried. Here, let me get that.' Lachlan jumped up off his seat and grabbed the mop and bucket she'd failed to put away the last time she'd mopped the floor.

Too tired to argue, she perched herself on the seat he'd just vacated and let him do the clean-up. It was mesmerising seeing the mop slosh the milk back and forth until it gradually disappeared. Almost as much as watching the flex of Lachlan's muscles as he brandished the mop.

'I needed something for the heartburn,' she blurted out. Though it was her blood pressure now that was causing the problem, her body clearly responding to the sight of him in a state of undress doing housework. A kink she didn't know she enjoyed until Lachlan had come back into her life.

Perhaps it was the nesting instinct to provide the perfect home for her baby that made a man doing chores all the more appealing. Although she wasn't sure she would be as excited to see anyone other than Lachlan doing it.

'There's not much milk left, I'm afraid.' He filled the bucket with hot water and a squirt of detergent before giving the floor one last clean.

'But I do have ice cream in the freezer,' she remembered, pulling out a tub of her favourite chocolate chip and fudge swirl, and grabbing two spoons.

'You think this will help us sleep?' he asked, taking the spoon she offered and peeling the lid off the tub.

'No, but it'll make staying awake more enjoyable. And I don't have to worry about getting fat.' She dug her spoon in and helped herself to a large scoop of chocolatey goodness.

'No, because it's all for the baby, right?' His smile suggested he didn't believe it at all, but was happy to let her indulge.

'Naturally.' She took another spoonful and savoured the creamy taste on her tongue. 'Mmm.'

When she glanced at Lachlan, she was sure he was watching her the way she'd looked at him earlier. Maybe it was wishful thinking, but she thought she'd seen a hunger there for more than ice cream. She shivered. A delicious chill of awareness skated across her skin that, despite her lack of make-up and the sight of her pigging out in the kitchen, he might still be attracted to her.

'Brain freeze? Maybe we should step away from the ice cream.'

Melissa nodded. It was better to have him take away her comfort food than let him think she was reading something more into this than sharing a tub of ice cream.

He put it back in the freezer and came back to sit beside her.

'Everything's all right,' she assured him, believing that her and the baby's welfare was the reason he'd been sitting here in the dark.

'I hope so.'

'I think it's just shaken us both up a little tonight.' Melissa lifted the spoons and moved over to the sink so he couldn't see her face. She didn't want to look at him when she told him her deepest fears, though she thought he needed to know he wasn't the only one scared about what the future held.

She let her hands rest on the soft swell of her belly, which was probably imperceptible to anyone else, but she liked to think she could feel her baby growing in there already.

'What is it, Melissa? What's bothering you?'

'That I'm going to be alone. I don't have my family to hold my hand or worry about me. I'm afraid my baby is going to end up as lonely as I am.' The second she admitted her fears, the tears fell from her eyes.

She'd tried to convince herself she could do all this on her own, but as time went on, it was becoming clear she was going to need support. Someone she could rely on. It was what she always suggested to her patients—that they made sure they had a good support system in place—and now she realised the truth in that advice.

Emotions, as well as hormones, were all over the place during pregnancy. It was important to have someone to lean on, to give pep talks when needed, a listening ear, and a hand to hold. Melissa didn't feel as though she had anyone willing to do that. At least, no one who wasn't doing it under duress.

'You both have me.' Lachlan's voice sounded low in her ear, sending the hairs on the back of her neck to attention. Then he slid his arms around her and rested his hands on top of hers. Covering her belly.

She wanted so desperately to believe him. He'd said it often enough, but unfortunately his actions didn't match his words.

'How can I believe that, Lachlan, when you seem so distant lately?' She didn't even dare mention the kiss in case it sent him running again.

He dropped his head. 'I'm truly sorry. I never meant to hurt you, or mess you around. It's just… I'm afraid of doing something we'll both regret.'

It took Melissa a moment to process what he was talking about. 'The kiss?'

'Yes, the kiss. There's six months until this

baby is born. I don't want to get into something now, only for it to fizzle out before the birth.'

'And I don't get a say in that? What about what I want?' Whatever did or didn't happen between them affected her too.

'I don't want to hurt you, Melissa, but more than anything, I want to be present in my baby's life. I can't jeopardise that for anyone. Not even you.'

It was difficult to hear, but it let Melissa know where she stood. She couldn't begrudge her unborn child taking priority in Lachlan's affections, when that's what she'd wanted. By telling him he was the father, she'd hoped deep down that he would step up and be the parent both she and the baby needed him to be. So their child didn't grow up feeling rejected the way they both had.

Still, it didn't stop her from needing to be a part of his life too. Especially when he made her feel the way he did. Even now, despite her upset, she was aware of him so close to her. Her fingers ached to touch the smooth skin of his chest. Her lips parted, ready to pick up from where their last kiss had ended. She still wanted him, wanted that same physical connection they'd shared at the festival. Even if it meant setting her feelings aside.

'Then why kiss me in the first place?' She didn't imagine Lachlan was the kind of man who couldn't control his impulses. After all, he'd managed to stay away from her for a week without any kind of contact.

Lachlan scrubbed his hands over his face. 'Because I wanted to. I like you, Melissa. You should know that at least. But what I want should come after what my baby needs. A father.'

'You don't think that part of what makes good parents is that they're happy? We both know there's an attraction between us, and I for one am tired of fighting it. It's exhausting pretending that I don't want to be with you. To relive what we had together at the music festival. Would it really be so bad to find some comfort in one another again?' When they'd first met, they'd been going through difficult, emotional times in their lives. Much like now. At least then they'd been able to forget everything outside of the bedroom for that night. She would like to have the opportunity to do the same now.

'Trust me, I want that too, Melissa. But

there's so much else at stake now…' The push and pull of his emotions was obvious in the way he was reaching out to her, but still trying to keep his distance. She recognised the turmoil tearing him apart inside, because she felt it too. What she wouldn't do to be that carefree couple who'd thrown caution to the wind once more. It might be the last time they'd get the chance to do that before they became parents for real.

'We don't have to make promises to one another of happy ever afters. Acting on this attraction doesn't have to affect how we parent this baby. I need you, Lachlan. Even if it's only for tonight.' Melissa reminded him of the time frame he'd originally suggested. Stepping outside of the boundaries they'd set up when they'd reconnected for one night didn't seem as scary as anything more serious and complicated.

What she was suggesting wasn't necessarily everything she wanted, but she'd learned it wasn't possible to have it all. She wanted him to hold her in his arms for a little while. All she needed for now was to know he wanted her. To feel loved, even if it didn't last beyond the morning. The fear of losing him was gradually being blotted out by the fear of never really showing how much they felt for one another.

Lachlan didn't believe what he was hearing. He'd been up all night worrying not only about what could have happened to Melissa and the baby, but what he was going to do about his feelings for her. The conflict between doing the right thing by his child and what he wanted was tearing him apart. The next six months, not to mention the rest of his life, trying to keep the two separate was going to severely test him. It wasn't that he didn't want to try with Melissa, but he was worried that if—*when*—it ended, it would affect his relationship with his child. The last thing he wanted.

This way it seemed they could have it all. At least temporarily.

'It would be nice just to be together without worrying about the consequences...' He was tired of overthinking, of fighting his feelings for Melissa, denying himself the chance to be with her.

Today, when he thought there was a possibility that he'd lose her, had proven to him just how strongly he felt about her.

'It's how we met, isn't it? We were able to enjoy each other without a commitment, or even knowing each other's surnames, if I recall.' She teased him with the memory, colour rising in her cheeks, and the twinkle in her eye a little brighter. The idea certainly seemed to appeal to her, and Lachlan could see the benefits. In fact, he was struggling to come up with any cons.

'Getting pregnant kind of forced our hand though.' If he hadn't moved to the city, or come to Claire's appointment, he'd still be none the wiser about the baby. They wouldn't even be in one another's orbit now, though he'd still be thinking about her and the time they'd spent together.

'So now we get to take control. Decide what we want to do, instead of letting consequences, or our consciences, dictate our actions.' She placed a hand in the middle of his chest, scorching his skin and awakening his weary body. There was no denying he wanted to be with her. He ached for her. It was the consequences of giving in to those urges he worried about. Especially when the last time had caused such a massive upheaval in both of their lives.

'Are you sure?' His resolve was weakening with each second she was touching him, making him forget everything except how she made him feel.

If only he could manage not to get too emotionally invested in them as a couple, it was probably the best he could hope for.

His heart was trying to convince his head this was a good idea.

Then Melissa stood up on her tiptoes and kissed him, and the decision was made for him. He took her hand, and she led him upstairs to her bedroom, not another word spoken between them. A silent agreement to embark on this bold adventure together.

He slowly unbuttoned his way down her nightshirt, her earlier confidence apparently subsiding as she bit her lip. There was a hitch in her breath as he uncovered her body to his gaze, but she had absolutely nothing to be nervous about. Of course, there were subtle changes to her body from the last time they'd been together because of the pregnancy, but she was incredibly beautiful.

Lachlan kissed her on the mouth. Long and deep, trying to block out any negative thoughts she might have over her changing body. He cupped her breast in his hand, fuller than he remembered, and when he sucked on her nipple, it was clearly more sensitive.

He pushed her nightdress off her shoulders so she was totally exposed to him. Saw the goose bumps rise on her flesh, and her pink nipples stand to attention against her pale skin. It was too much to resist.

He kissed her hard, gripped her backside as he lifted her off the ground and wrapped her legs around his waist. His erection fought to escape the confines of his boxers as he pressed between her thighs, her soft heat teasing him through the thin fabric. He walked them over to the bed and laid her down gently, treating her like the precious cargo she was.

Though Melissa clearly wasn't feeling fragile when she reached between their bodies and stroked the length of his manhood, making him suck in a breath.

'I've missed you.' He buried his face in the side of her neck, kissing and nibbling his way along. Inhaling the sweet scent he'd been without for what seemed like an eternity.

'I've missed you too.' She slid her hands under the waistband of his underwear and grabbed his backside, leaving him in no doubt about that.

Melissa pushed his boxers down, baring

him completely, and leaving their prone bodies skin to skin in the most intimate contact. It was torture and heaven all at once.

She took him in hand again and squeezed firmly, making his entire body tremble and his resolve shatter. Clearly she wanted him as much as he wanted her, and it had been way too long since the last time they'd done this. When he was with her, he felt whole again. One hundred percent masculine.

Lachlan claimed her with one thrust. Her gasp, his cry of triumph. He didn't want to think of her being anyone else's, even though the nature of this arrangement made it a possibility somewhere down the line.

Melissa slid her arms around his neck and pulled him down for a kiss. At the same time, she tightened her inner muscles around him, completely scrambling his brain and overwhelming him with sensations. All of them pleasant.

He loved her body, the way she made him feel, the connection they had. He loved…this. Lachlan was too afraid to continue down that emotional path and pushed inside her again so he couldn't finish the thought. Instead, he was completely consumed by the physical feeling of being with her. Those sensations he could allow himself to experience.

His hips drove home his insistence again, indulging his needs, and bringing Melissa closer to the edge with every move. Her building moans of ecstasy fuelled his pace, as well as his ego. He wanted her to feel as good as he did. For this to be as good for her as it was for him. Then she'd want to do it again and again, and there'd be room for him in her life in some safe capacity.

Melissa was the mother of his baby, the woman who'd made him feel like a man again, and he didn't want to lose her. He was just afraid that he'd want her too much.

The sound of her climax echoed around the bedroom, the shockwaves reverberating through his body from hers until he couldn't fight it any longer. It was the one moment when he didn't have to hold back. He poured all of those feelings for her he was afraid to say out loud into her with a roar. Until his limbs were shaking with the effort, and his breath came in heavy pants.

His chest rapidly rose and fell in synch with Melissa's as they recovered. Lying side by side, grinning at each other as though they'd won the lottery. In most people's books, he already had, starting a family with an amazing woman who still wanted to share a bed with him. The problem was that he wanted it all, but had enough experience to know that wasn't possible. He had to sacrifice something to make it work. If it had to be a proper relationship with Melissa, then that's what he would forfeit if it meant their child would grow up in a stable environment with two present parents.

He could give his love to their baby, but he couldn't risk giving it to Melissa when there was just too much to lose.

CHAPTER EIGHT

'MORNING.'

Melissa blinked awake at the sound of Lachlan's voice, wondering if she was still half-asleep.

'Morning,' she croaked.

'There wasn't much in the way of food in the cupboards. This was the best I could come up with. I can go grab a few things from the shops if you need anything?' He set a tray with orange juice, hot buttered toast and a bowl of cereal on the bed, and hovered expectantly.

'No. I'll get shopping in later. Sit down and help me eat this.' She moved the tray aside and pulled the covers back so he could get in beside her.

He was beaming as he helped himself to a slice of toast from the stack he'd piled high on the plate. Melissa took a sip of juice before tucking into some sugary cereal, certain she needed the energy boost after last night's antics between the sheets.

She hadn't expected Lachlan to even be here this morning, never mind make her breakfast. It was considerate of him, but not the actions of a man who was only here for the sex. She was glad he'd stayed the night, and well into the morning.

It was good to see him happy and a pleasant way to start the working day. At least neither of them felt the need to run away after giving in to temptation this time. And what fun it had been to simply enjoy being together!

Their first time together definitely hadn't been a fluke. They had a chemistry she'd never had in the years she'd been with Chris. An understanding of what they both needed, and a passion that fizzed in her veins with every kiss, every touch. It was a wonder they'd held out for as long as they had under the circumstances. At least this time they didn't have to worry about the consequences, because the baby was already on the way. It gave them more of a sense of freedom, even if she had to keep her feelings in check.

That soppy expression on his face was adorable, and Melissa could only imagine how he would look seeing his own baby for the first time.

Now that the initial shock had worn off, and she was sure Lachlan would stick around for his baby, she was beginning to look forward to the arrival too. Only time would tell if she and Lachlan would do this again. It mightn't be such fun against the backdrop of a crying baby, lack of sleep, and dirty nappies. They might struggle like any other couple with a newborn, even though they weren't actually together in the conventional sense.

So they should probably make the most of the time they had together now in case it all came to an end too soon.

'You know, in a few months, I'm going to be the size of a house. We mightn't be able to do this any more. You mightn't want to.'

Lachlan set down what was left of his toast and cradled her head in his hands. 'I will always want you. You will always be beautiful to me.' He kissed her, reawakening that need for him inside her.

Last night together had been special. Hot. She supposed because she'd suggested keeping things purely physical, he hadn't needed to hold back, or worry about her feelings. In that way, it was much like their time at the festival. For her, the thrill was in simply being with him. Kissing him. Touching him. Having him in her life, and her bed, in any capacity.

Perhaps that was pitiful, being so lonely she'd settled for sex, rather than run the risk of chasing him away if she admitted she had feelings for him as more than the baby's father. He wasn't just a convenient bed partner. Lachlan had become an important, present part of her life. But she couldn't tell him that. Not when he was so afraid personal feelings would affect how he'd relate to his child.

Melissa wanted to believe he'd always want her, that he'd still think she was beautiful when she couldn't see her own feet past her belly. But like their time together, nothing was promised forever.

She kissed him back, wanting to block out all of those negative thoughts. If she only had him for a little while to herself, could only have this until it became uncomfortable physically and emotionally, then she'd enjoy it while it lasted.

She moved the breakfast things to her bedside table, hungrier for Lachlan than a piece of toast. He was certainly more satisfying.

With a confidence she had to dig deep for, Melissa pushed him back onto the mattress and straddled him. She was still naked, and aware the morning sunlight shining in through the window wasn't going to hide any imperfections. But she needed to convince him, as well as herself, that she could brazen this out.

'Feeling frisky this morning, are we?' Lachlan asked with a grin, grabbing her by the hips.

'Only when a man brings me breakfast in bed.'

'I'll have to make sure I do it more often, then,' he said, lifting his head to kiss her thoroughly.

The promise that this wasn't going to be a one-off after all only made her want him more. Melissa ground against him, testing herself as much as Lachlan. He pressed his thumb intimately against her, teasing, stretching, playing with her until they were both coated with her arousal. He slid easily into her then, filling her completely, as their bodies joined together.

She rocked her hips as he thrust up to meet her again and again, wishing they could stay like this forever. Where happiness was guaranteed and neither of them wanted to be anywhere else.

* * *

Lachlan was reluctant to leave Melissa's bed. It was too cosy, too tempting to give up everything to stay there with her and pretend the rest of the world didn't exist, and there were no reasons why they couldn't be together.

Unfortunately, they had to work to earn a living, and he was going to have a family to provide for soon.

'Why don't we have dinner when we're both free?'

'Sounds good.'

'I'll pick you up tomorrow about eight o'clock, then.' Lachlan leaned in and gave her a kiss.

He still needed to go home and get showered and changed before his shift. It was supposed to have been nothing more than a goodbye peck on the lips. But it soon developed into something more. Every touch between them seemed to be the catalyst for a greater chemical reaction. They slid their arms around one another, pressing their bodies tightly together as they deepened the kiss, bringing back vivid memories of everything they'd got up to in her bed last night.

It was like this every time. That was probably why he'd tried, and failed, to keep things between them to a minimum recently. He'd known his feelings for Melissa were growing stronger, and he'd been worried that by facing them, he was inevitably going to let her and the baby down if things didn't work out. Last night had been unexpected, and eye-opening.

They'd been vulnerable, the worry over the baby bonding them, making them cling to one another for comfort. He'd let his defences down, the thought of potentially losing Melissa or the baby drowning out any misgivings he had about being close to her. It had been nice to leave all of his worries aside for one night, having spent too long living on tenterhooks about what the future held because of his illness and becoming a father. Having the freedom to be with Melissa and simply enjoy their time together was something he could get used to. It also made him wonder if he should stop overanalysing everything in his life and learn to live in the moment when there was apparently so much to be gained. Certainly, he wanted to be able to do this again if he had the chance.

The dreaded alarm sounded from his phone, reminding him that he had to get out of bed, and he responded with a groan.

'I'm going to be late for work if I don't get a move on,' he muttered against Melissa's lips.

'I can give you a lift.' Melissa went to sit up, clutching the sheets to her naked body, but Lachlan pulled her back down beside him on the bed.

'No. You stay here and rest. I'll get my run in before work. It's not too far from here to my place.' Whilst it was true that he didn't want to inconvenience her, he also wanted to remember her lying here like this. It kept thoughts of the real world, and what complications their night together could bring, at bay for a while longer. In this room, he could pretend this was their whole universe.

'If you're sure, I could do with another forty winks before I go in. I didn't get a whole lot of sleep last night.' Melissa's coy glance almost tempted him to stay, but her yawn reminded him that she needed sleep more.

'You rest. I'll text you later.' He gave her one last kiss before forcing himself to get up and grab his clothes.

She watched him dress, though her eyes were already beginning to close.

'I can't wait until our dinner,' she said through another yawn.

Neither could he, and therein lay the problem. The highlight of his days was being with her, and there was nothing remotely casual about his feelings for her.

In an ideal world, they'd be madly in love, raising this baby together in their home. He was beginning to wonder why that picture had to remain pure fantasy when they both seemed so happy together.

CHAPTER NINE

MELISSA MANAGED A quick change out of her uniform before Lachlan picked her up at work. He greeted her with a kiss on the cheek before taking her bag and placing it on the back seat of his car. She climbed into the front, glad he was driving since her nerves were getting the better of her at the prospect of another night with him. He'd been on her mind all day, along with thoughts of everything they'd done together.

'Are you sure you don't want a beer? I can drive us back.' Melissa knew if she could partake in some alcohol tonight, she would. For some reason, going out for dinner with Lachlan seemed more intimate than the time they'd spent in bed together, or the fact that they were going to be co-parents.

It marked a change in their relationship that part of her had hoped for, but that also brought more anxiety. Yesterday had been emotional and challenging, and apparently the catalyst for giving in to temptation again. They hadn't discussed what came next for them as a couple. If that's what they were now. But maybe that was for the best. What had happened the other night had been organic, and she didn't want to tarnish where they were by overanalysing everything again.

Those fears that Lachlan would leave her were always going to be there, regardless of whether she admitted she had feelings for him or not. Maybe she should just let herself enjoy their time together for what it was now, and see where it would lead…

'It's fine. I should keep a clear head if we're going to discuss childcare arrangements. Plus, I want other parts of me wide awake if we decide to make a night of it.' He shot her a lingering glance as though waiting for confirmation that she was agreeable.

Even the thought of sharing her bed with him again was getting her hot under the collar—and everywhere else. If it wasn't for the fact that she was responsible for the baby's nutritional needs as well as her own, she would've been tempted to tell him to forget dinner altogether and head straight home.

Instead, she simply reached across the front

of the car and gave his thigh a squeeze, hoping that was enough to persuade him she was more than agreeable to the suggestion. Her reward came with the feel of his muscles bunching under her fingertips, and the visible clenching of his jaw. She gave a triumphant smile at the thought that she'd managed to get him as aroused as she currently was at the prospect of the night ahead.

'I haven't eaten since midday, so I'm looking forward to a good meal. None of that fancy fine dining stuff that wouldn't fill a hole in your tooth, you know. A proper plate of food. Are you hungry too?' Lachlan kept his eyes trained on the road straight ahead, and his sudden rambling, hardly pausing for breath, amused Melissa. It felt very much as though he was trying to steer his mind somewhere other than her touch, or spending the night together, when it was he who'd conjured the thought in the first place.

'Starved,' she said, willing him to turn around and see the desire she was sure was shining in her eyes for him.

The shaky breath he let out told her he could sense it.

Flashing orange lights up ahead in the darkness caught Melissa's attention, and Lachlan began to slow the car down.

'There's something going on…' he said, peering closely through the windscreen.

The rear lights of the cars ahead blazed brightly as they hit the brakes, traffic eventually coming to a halt. A flurry of activity around them and people rushing out of their cars suggested something serious had happened, putting all thoughts of romantic rendezvous out of Melissa's head for now. Lachlan's too, it seemed, as he pulled the handbrake on, switched off the engine, and undid his seat belt.

'I'll see what's going on. Someone might be hurt.'

She supposed it was his paramedic training kicking in that compelled him to help, and she wouldn't sit idly by if someone was hurt either. Lachlan likely expected her to wait, but that wasn't Melissa. Instead, she grabbed her midwife bag from the back seat in case there was anything in there that could help, and headed off after him.

It was a set of temporary traffic lights which had initially slowed traffic, but cars remained at a standstill even after the green light showed, and it was easy to see why.

Heavy machinery involved in the roadworks had toppled into a ditch at the side of the road, but the panicked shouting confirmed it was more serious than a damaged digger.

Lachlan didn't hesitate to climb down and assess the scene, whilst Melissa took her time, making sure she didn't slip on any loose dirt. She didn't miss the look of disapproval on Lachlan's face as he reached out a hand to make sure she got onto safe ground, but rushed to cut him off before he could scold her.

'Don't start. We're both medical professionals, and I have some first aid supplies in my bag.'

In a sign that he knew her well enough not to argue, Lachlan simply led her over to the men in high visibility jackets and hard hats gathered around the upturned digger.

Lachlan introduced himself to the workmen. 'Hey, I'm Lachlan McNairn. I'm an off-duty paramedic. Is there anything I can do?'

'I've phoned for an ambulance, but one of our guys, Paul, is trapped under there. I don't know what happened. Maybe the road weakened and gave way… The driver got out, but Paul was digging in the ditch. Are we right to move this?' Lachlan assumed the man speaking was the foreman, since he was keen to place the blame elsewhere and was standing back watching as the rest of the men were attempting to shift the digger bucket, which appeared to have Paul pinned down.

'Yes.' If the weight was lifted after any more than fifteen minutes, it could lead to crush injury syndrome, a potentially life-threatening condition. Removing that pressure could release toxins into the system and overwhelm the kidneys, causing renal failure. There was also the possibility of the change in chemical balance leading to cardiac arrest.

He added his weight to the effort to shift the load off Paul's chest, and with a lot of grunting and straining muscles, they managed it. The man lying on the ground was deathly pale, but he was conscious.

'I—I can't breathe,' Paul managed through gasps.

'Don't try to talk. We need to see what damage has been done.' Lachlan set to work with his preliminary assessment of the man's condition. He was conscious and breathing, though it was clearly laboured.

'I might be able to help until the ambulance gets here.' Melissa came down beside him and rummaged in her bag to produce a manual re-suscitator, a self-inflating bag used to deliver positive pressure ventilation.

'Thanks.' Lachlan shot her an appreciative glance, letting her get on with assisting Paul's breathing so he could continue checking the rest of the man's injuries.

Although Melissa was a midwife, she would have first aid training, and he was grateful she was willing to help.

'How long has he been trapped?' he asked the crew.

'About five minutes. Not long.' Someone answered.

'Good.' Lachlan turned his attention back to the injured man. 'Paul? I just need you to point to where the pain is.'

He lifted a shaky arm and patted his chest.

'Nowhere else?' There was always the concern that there could be internal damage.

Paul shook his head.

Lachlan wished he had his usual equipment to hand so he could run an echocardiogram. With crush injuries, there was a chance of hy-perkalaemia occurring—elevated potassium levels—and changes in these levels could be identified in this way, helping to give a better assessment of the situation, and therefore better hospital treatment after transfer. All he could do in these circumstances was keep the man as comfortable as possible and let the ambulance crew take over when they got here.

'We'll give you something for the pain, but you're going to need some X-rays. You might have some fractured ribs. We'll know better when we get you to hospital.' It was obvious Paul was in pain, his chest tender and badly bruised, but they wouldn't be able to see what was going on inside until he had a scan.

Paul pushed the mask off his face, beginning to come round a bit more thanks to Melissa's intervention. 'Am I going to die?'

'Hopefully you'll just need to rest up for a while.' It was a question Lachlan was often asked, and one he didn't like to answer when there were so many variables in medical emergencies. What seemed like a straightforward accident could end up with a fractured rib puncturing a lung and effectively drowning a patient. It was his job, therefore, to stabilise the injured party and watch him closely until they could get specialist medical care. Like the rest of his life, it meant he was tasked with a great deal of responsibility.

'We're going to have a baby,' Paul said, a smile lighting up his pale features.

Lachlan exchanged a conspiratorial smile with Melissa, knowing they shared the same secret.

'Congratulations. Now just lie still for me.' Lachlan knew something about wanting to tell the world about impending fatherhood. These last couple of weeks, he'd wanted to do the same. The baby no longer seemed like an inconvenience, but something he wanted to boast about. Whilst trying to navigate their path to parenthood, he and Melissa had yet to go public about him being the father of her baby.

He'd drawn enough awkward questions from his family trying to explain the set-up. It did make him wonder about when the baby arrived. Of course, he'd want people to know he was the father when he was determined to be a permanent part of his child's life. He wasn't sure how Melissa intended to handle that, and it was one of the things they needed to discuss.

'We've been trying for years to start a family. They're my whole world. I don't want to leave them now.' Like Paul, Lachlan was beginning to realise he wanted to be here for his family as long as possible.

What he didn't want was to be emotionally

absent, afraid to open himself completely to her and the baby in case he didn't live up to expectations. Perhaps being recognised as the father publicly would help him feel more part of that. What last night had made him realise was that it was pointless pretending he didn't already care for Melissa or the baby. It was only hurting everyone maintaining a distance because of things that might happen, that ultimately he had no control over.

'That's not going to happen, Paul. You'll see your wife soon.' He broke his usual stance to offer his patient some comfort, convincing himself it was better to give him something to look forward to than worry himself into a worse condition.

Advice he should probably take on board himself. He was so consumed by the thought of the mistakes he might make, it was possible he was missing out on something really special. Their pasts had prevented him and Melissa from exploring all aspects of a relationship, but he knew they had a special bond that went beyond impending parenthood. If they could be brave enough, there was a chance they could be more than good parents. They could be a family.

Every day Melissa became a greater part

of his life, and she showed him more of the amazing woman she was. Even now, she tended to the superficial cuts on Paul's face, cleaning him up with antiseptic wipes and dressing the deeper wounds he'd sustained in the accident, highlighting her caring nature. This was going above and beyond her role as a midwife, and he knew it was part of who she was. Something that wasn't taught or learned from textbooks. In that moment, he knew she would be there for him should the worst ever happen.

It was down to him to be there for her until it did.

Thankfully, the sound of the ambulance sirens filled the night air, and it wasn't long before two of his colleagues were climbing down the bank to reach them. He gave them a quick rundown of Paul's injuries. Then, as carefully and as gently as they could, they moved him onto a stretcher and got him into the ambulance.

'I'll phone your wife, Paul,' the foreman called as the paramedics closed the doors. 'And thanks for all of your help too.'

'No problem.' Lachlan shook his hand, then assisted Melissa in picking up the debris from the first aid they'd administered on site. Once she'd repacked her bag, he gave her a hand back up onto the road.

She was shivering so hard he could hear her teeth chattering once they were in the car.

'You're freezing. I shouldn't have kept you standing around in the cold for so long.' He grabbed the jacket he'd tossed onto the back seat earlier and reached across to tuck it in around her shoulders.

'I make my own decisions, Lachlan.' She didn't need to give him the side-eye for him to realise that. Melissa had been doing that since the day he met her, and he admired her for it. He hadn't been able to act on his gut feelings without considering every consequence thanks to his father's actions and the impact they'd had on those around him.

Lachlan hoped the fact that he'd made a few more spontaneous decisions proved what a positive influence she was having on him. Maybe someday he'd be able to accept his father's actions and open himself up to the life he could have if he wasn't so worried about turning out like him.

'I'll put the heat on anyway. I'm feeling the chill myself now.' He turned the temperature dial on full while they waited for the traffic to begin moving again.

'It was probably only adrenaline keeping us warm out there,' she said with a smile. Then with more concern added, 'I hope he's going to be okay.'

Lachlan reached out and squeezed her hand. 'I'm sure he will be.'

Perhaps it was the bond he felt with someone else about to be a dad with an uncertain future ahead, but there was something illogical inside him that said if things worked out for Paul, everything would be okay for him too. And he wanted that more than anything. But how could he put her through the pain and suffering his treatment had caused him and his loved ones the first time around if his cancer returned? All he could do was keep his fingers crossed for him and Paul.

'You were impressive back there, taking charge and keeping him calm.' She yawned and leaned her head against his shoulder. It was a sign of how comfortable things between them had become now that they'd stopped fighting whatever feelings kept drawing them together. He should've been disconcerted by the fact that they were so close when he'd done his best to avoid that until last night. Except it was kind of nice. It was easy to imagine a different life, one where he was free of cancer and didn't have to worry about abandoning anyone. Where they could be driving home with their baby in the back seat. A nice, normal family life. The one he never had, and never thought he would have.

'You were pretty impressive yourself. We can reward ourselves with some carb-laden food at the restaurant. I'm sure they'll still be holding our table.' He'd already seen how Melissa handled her role as a midwife, but tonight had highlighted how supportive she was in general. It was nice to have her there for backup, to share the load with someone. Ironic, when that was the very thing he'd been trying to run away from. Determined to do everything on his own.

'Actually, I don't have much of an appetite any more. I'm just tired. Do you mind if we go home instead?' Another yawn hit the point home.

'Sure.' He headed towards Melissa's house, and it wasn't long before her steady breathing signified her lapse into sleep.

When they pulled up outside her house, he touched her gently on the shoulder. 'Hey. We're here.'

Melissa lifted her head and stretched out her neck. 'You want to come in?'

'I should probably let you get some sleep.'

'It's okay. You wanted to talk about the baby.'

'We can do that anytime. It's been an exhausting night, and you need to rest.' He wanted to take care of her, even if that only meant making sure she got enough sleep.

She undid her seat belt and got out of the car, not giving him time to argue. 'It's fine, Lachlan. Talking isn't going to tire me out.'

He wasn't so sure, but he followed her into the house regardless.

Once inside, Melissa kicked off her shoes and curled up on the sofa. It seemed like the most natural thing in the world to sit there with her. He lifted her feet and placed them on his lap to give her a massage.

'Mmm. That feels so good.' She closed her eyes, making little moans of satisfaction that didn't fail to call to his basest needs. Tonight, however, there were more important things to deal with than his libido.

'Glad I can do something for you.'

'You do a lot for me, Lachlan.'

'I hope so, and I want to do the same for the baby.'

'That's what you want to talk about?'

'Yes. I guess I just want to know what my role is going to be.'

Melissa frowned at him. 'Well, you're the dad.'

It sounded so simple when put like that, but he knew having a title alone didn't mean anything. 'Yes, but I also want to be a father. And not just an every-other-weekend one.'

'Okay.' She sat up straight, and he hoped he hadn't gone too far in voicing his wants for the future. It was a topic they'd tried to avoid, because it likely meant facing whatever feelings they had for one another too at some point. Something he knew terrified them both, opening up their hearts and sharing their lives with someone again.

'I want to be actively involved. That means sharing the childcare equally, school runs when the time comes, parent-teacher meetings, holidays… I want to be there for all of it.' He meant that. Lachlan had no intention of shuffling off the earth anytime soon, and since he was trying to be the father he never had, he wanted to be there as much as possible in his child's life.

Melissa sat quietly, taking it all in. Probably contemplating the implications of that in her life. Only time would tell if the risk was worth taking, but now, from his point of view, they had to try and make it work for the baby's sake. Neither of them wanted the baby to suffer as a result of their personal issues.

Eventually she said, 'I'm sure we can come to an arrangement. I want to get back to work at some point, so having you on board would really help.'

That was easier than he'd expected, maybe because of the time they had been spending together.

'Great. So, we can make it official, then? It's okay for me to tell people I'm the dad?' Perhaps he'd been holding back on that too, afraid that once he acknowledged it outside of family, it made everything more real. Now that he and Melissa were working through their own hang-ups, however, he thought it was about time he went all in. Stopped holding back, and focused on the good things in his life instead of waiting for the worst to happen.

'Well, I'm okay with that if you are. It doesn't make any sense to sneak around pretending otherwise. I mean, we don't have to take out a full-page ad in the paper or anything, but feel free to share the news.'

She seemed at ease with the idea now. A

far cry from those early days when she hadn't even wanted to tell him she was pregnant in the first place. It showed how far they'd come already.

'Thank you. Hopefully things will get easier for us from now on.' He didn't dare hope for too much, but he was enjoying just being in the moment with Melissa. That was enough for now.

'I hope so. Now, can we go to bed?' Melissa got up off the sofa and took his hand.

Lachlan let her lead him towards the bedroom, not caring if they spent the night making love or if she went straight to sleep. All that mattered was that she was in his arms. It had become so natural, comfortable, to be together like this, that he wished it wouldn't end. He didn't want to think about the reasons they shouldn't let their defences down when the alternative was so enjoyable.

CHAPTER TEN

MELISSA AND LACHLAN had had a couple of weeks of sneaking in and out of each other's beds, exchanging sexy texts and phone calls, and generally enjoying a passionate adventure together. Who knew how long it would last, but the intensity they shared in the bedroom showed no sign of abating. Nor did the feelings she had towards him. If anything, they were growing every day.

Along with their stolen moments together, and hot sultry nights, they were also becoming closer on a familial level. That's why she'd agreed to come to Claire's house tonight to celebrate the birth of her baby with the rest of Lachlan's family.

Melissa had met his mother a couple of times during postnatal visits, when they were visiting Claire. A potentially awkward situation apparently negated by the fact that his mother seemed to like her.

Lachlan wanted her to get to know his family so that when their baby came, they would feel a part of it. An idea she was on board with, since she'd grown up without an extended family. She wanted their baby to have people to turn to when needed. Something she hadn't had for a long time herself before Chris came along.

Perhaps she'd been guilty of clinging on to him in place of the parents she was missing at the time. He'd been a good man, but she hadn't felt about him the way she felt about Lachlan.

That was why, although she was enjoying this time with Lachlan, she was more worried than ever about being abandoned again. She'd been devastated by Chris's death when it happened, but she and Lachlan were about to become a family. Chris had never been as enthusiastic about the idea of becoming a father as Lachlan was. They were making plans for the future as parents, and given their current situation, it wasn't unreasonable to believe they could have a relationship beyond that. She had so much more to lose if Lachlan disappeared out of her life the way Chris and her parents had.

Although she may have seemed nonchalant about agreeing to Lachlan's want to be so involved in family life, it was so she didn't scare him off. Melissa didn't want him to feel as though it was a big deal to her, even though it was. It marked a turning point in their relationship, evidence that she was putting her trust in him not to break her heart.

Melissa rang the doorbell, her pulse racing, her palms sweating. Although she'd been to Claire's house on many occasions to check on her and the baby, this wasn't a professional visit. This was a 'meet the family' scenario.

'Hi, Melissa. Come on in. Is my brother not with you?' Claire opened the door with the baby in one arm.

'He got delayed at the hospital, but he'll be here as soon as he can.' When Lachlan had phoned Melissa to tell her he'd be late, her heart had sunk, knowing she'd have to come here on her own and meet everyone without him.

She followed Claire down the hall and into the living room, where her senses were assaulted by the sights and sounds of the family gathering. The loud chattering and laughter mixed with the happy squeals of children were overwhelming. When she was growing up as an only child, the house had been quiet save for the occasional friend she had over. She wasn't used to this level of noise, or the number of people gathered in one small room.

Once she got over the initial shock, she supposed it must've been nice to grow up surrounded by a big family like this, and wondered if their child would be part of it or remain hovering on the outside like her.

'Everyone! This is Melissa.' Claire announced her arrival to the room, refusing her the opportunity to back out.

'Hi.' Under the spotlight of the communal gaze, Melissa gave a little wave. Not knowing what else was expected of her.

Suddenly she was swamped with handshakes and introductions as the family came to introduce themselves.

'I'm Duncan, Lachlan's little brother. Claire and Mum have talked so much about you.'

'I'm Charlie.'

'And I'm Ava.'

The most adorable children sidled up to Melissa, and she bent down to say hello.

'It's lovely to meet you. I'm Melissa.'

'You're uncle Lachlan's friend,' the older boy with the beautiful brown curls said matter-of-factly.

'Yes.'

'Give her some space to breathe, guys. Why don't you come through to the kitchen with me, Melissa, and I'll get you something to drink.' Claire shooed everyone away, and though she wasn't thirsty, Melissa followed her, glad of a little breathing room.

The fact that she was wishing Lachlan was here for support, to ground her and stop her from becoming too anxious, said she'd already fallen too deep. She was relying on him too much. Attached to the idea of them being a couple. Already starting to think of them as a family.

'Thanks for that. I'm not used to big family gatherings.'

'Yes, Lachlan said you're an only child and your parents live in Florida. Hold her for a minute, will you?' Claire handed the baby over before Melissa had the chance to reply, and began to pour out two glasses of wine from the many bottles littering the kitchen counter.

Melissa stared down at Lachlan's niece, feeling a surge of love for the little bundle sucking on her tiny fist. She always got broody over babies, but there was something extra special about this one. Whether it was because this baby was part of Lachlan's family, or from the vain hope that they could one day be related, Melissa couldn't be sure.

'Don't worry, it's non-alcoholic.' Claire nudged a glass towards Melissa and took one herself.

'Thanks.' The sweet sparkling grape juice was refreshing, and Melissa made a note to stock up on some herself, since she wouldn't be drinking anything alcoholic for the foreseeable future.

'We haven't really had a chance to talk since I found out you're having my brother's baby.'

Melissa almost choked on her drink at the thought that she was about to get a lecture from one of her patients. It had been something of a blessing that they'd only really seen each other on a professional level, often when her mother was in attendance, and the focus was always on the welfare of Claire and her baby, Melanie. There hadn't been a chance for her to quiz Melissa on her 'intentions' towards Lachlan, or the nature of their relationship.

'I know. It's not an ideal situation for either of us, but we'll try our best to be good parents.' She hoped that was vague enough that Claire would realise she didn't want to talk about her personal life. Apart from not wanting to jinx what they did have, it wasn't something she was ready to discuss with anyone. Including Lachlan.

They hadn't defined what their relationship was or what expectations they had. Likely because they'd have to face up to the fact that it probably wasn't a good idea. Neither of them was ready to do that when they were enjoying each other so much without all of the agonising over what it meant for them to be together. If they did stop to focus on the repercussions, it might all be over.

There was a commotion from the living room, saving her from having to respond further. The kitchen door opened and Lachlan walked in, sending Melissa's heart racing upon seeing him.

'Hi, bro.' It was Claire who greeted him first.

'Hey, you two. Should my ears be burning?' He frowned, glancing between Melissa and Claire, aware that he'd walked in on a serious discussion.

'I was just telling Melissa you need some baby practice. Could you change Melanie whilst I dish out the hot food?' Claire unloaded her daughter into Lachlan's arms, grabbed the changing bag, and slung it over Melissa's shoulder.

'Your sister doesn't take no for an answer, does she?'

'Generally, she doesn't wait around for an answer. Shall we go upstairs where it's quieter? I don't want an audience.' Clearly not one to hang around for a response either, Lachlan turned and walked out of the kitchen. Since Melissa had all the nappy-changing essentials, she didn't have any choice but to follow. She supposed it would give them some privacy away from his family to talk too.

They walked back through the living room towards the stairs, barely drawing a glance. The novelty of their arrival had seemingly worn off, with everyone's attention now on the table of food. It wasn't a bad thing if it meant she would no longer be under scrutiny from the rest of the family.

Lachlan walked into the pretty pink nursery room and set Melanie down on the waist-high changing table. 'Okay, gorgeous girl, let's get you all cleaned up.'

Melissa took out the baby wipes and nappies and handed them over, watching him get soppy over his baby niece. He moved deftly to take off the wet nappy and clean the baby up, all the while talking in a soft sing-song voice. He was going to make a good dad.

Despite her own experience dealing with babies, she let him do the change. Lachlan looked good with a baby in his arms.

'I hope work wasn't too harrowing for you tonight,' she said, noting he'd been held up. That usually meant there'd been complications.

Lachlan looked at her as though he had no idea what she was talking about.

'The hospital…' she prompted him.

'Oh. No. I wasn't working.'

It was Melissa's turn to be confused. 'But I thought—'

'I was at the hospital, but it wasn't because of work.' The clench of his jaw and the furrow of a frown told her something was wrong.

Melissa's stomach lurched with that feeling of foreboding she'd hoped never to experience again. 'Then why?'

'Let me put this one down in her cot for a sleep. Then we'll talk.'

She wasn't sure she really wanted to know the answer, but neither did she want him to keep anything from her. Surprises in her life tended to be unpleasant, life-changing dramas. Apart from the pregnancy, of course, but she could do without any more plot twists.

Lachlan placed the baby in her cot, waiting until she was settled before walking away, and led Melissa out into the hallway. He closed the door behind him and took a moment before he spoke. Everything in his body language told her he didn't have good news to share with her.

'Lachlan? What is it?' She could barely get the words out past the ball of fear lodged in her throat.

'I—I had the results of my most recent check-up today. I didn't tell you I was going because I didn't want it preying on your mind. But they're not happy with the bloods. The tumour marker tests showed some proteins usually made by testicular cancer cells. I had to have more blood work today. It's probably nothing, but, you know, there's always that worry.'

She did know. Her insides were tied in knots right now despite his attempt to reassure her it was nothing untoward. It was admirable of him to be concerned about her when no doubt he was going through emotional hell himself. Cancer was a tough journey, physically and mentally, and the prospect of facing it twice must've been horrific.

She felt selfish that after her concern for him, her thoughts turned to her own self-preservation, but this was a lot to process. 'So what happens next?'

'I guess I'll find out soon. They won't wait around if they think the cancer's back in case it spreads. Probably a whole battery of tests, scans…at worst, more surgery and chemo.' The more he spoke about it, the more deflated he sounded, and the more Melissa's heart sank.

If the cancer had returned, it most certainly could have spread, and the outcome might not be as favourable as the last time. Not only was he facing months of uncertainty, but there was a possibility he wouldn't survive. At the very least, he would be exhausted, sick, and no longer the Lachlan she knew now. He'd told her himself the cancer had made him reassess his life, and he'd ended his last relationship. One way or another, he was going to leave her. Sticking around, waiting for it to happen, falling for him more every day, was only going to increase her pain when he inevitably did go.

She hated that she was even feeling this way at a time when he would need her most, but she had to think about the baby as well as herself. Whatever happened, he wasn't going to be here to share the parenting, and she knew she couldn't cope with looking after him as well as a child. She wasn't heartless, but she was afraid. Losing Chris had broken her, and losing Lachlan would be even worse when they were about to embark on their family journey. All she could think of was getting out now before the cancer killed them both.

'I'm so sorry, Lachlan.'

'Hey. It's not your fault.' His lopsided smile only made this harder.

'You're going through a lot.' She cleared her throat, trying to hold herself together. 'I think… I think perhaps we should cool things down between us so you can focus on your health.'

'It might be nothing, Melissa.'

'And I hope that's true for your sake, but my priority has to be the baby. I think I'd forgotten that in all of the excitement. You have your family to rally around you, but I—I just can't do this again.'

'What about the baby?' The look of hurt

in his eyes was unbearable, but the least she owed him was some reassurance there.

'If you're up to it, you can still be involved with the baby, but we should end whatever it is we've been doing. We both have other priorities.' She marvelled at her ability to sound calm and rational, when inside she was screaming. It seemed she was doomed to never have the love she craved from anyone, but she'd rather be alone than face losing her heart along with Lachlan. She could only hope that with some space, it wouldn't hurt as much.

'You're really doing this now?' The accusation in his voice was justified. They were in the wrong place, at the worst possible time for her to realise she should never have got involved with him.

'We can talk over arrangements for the baby later, but I think I need to go now. There's no point in dragging things out or making things any more awkward around your family than they already are. I'll make my excuses and leave. Don't follow me.'

She practically stumbled out of the room, tears already blurring her vision, and her legs barely holding her up. The last thing she saw before she left was Lachlan looking at her as though she'd torn his heart out of his chest with her bare hands.

Melissa didn't know how she was going to survive without him.

CHAPTER ELEVEN

'WE'VE GOT A road traffic accident involving a pregnant woman,' Scot told Lachlan as he climbed into the ambulance.

'Then what are we waiting for?' Every time a mother and child were in danger he was going to think about Melissa and his baby.

Embarking on a relationship with her had been a big commitment for him, one he hadn't taken lightly. The days, and nights, they'd spent together had convinced him that they had a future as a family. He'd thought he'd made a breakthrough, letting go of his hang-ups about being around forever to focus on everything he had in the present. Or everything he'd thought he had. Perhaps he'd got so wrapped up in the idea of having Melissa and the baby permanently in his life, he'd been blinded to the fact that she wasn't as invested. They'd never had a conversation about being a couple, but he'd taken for granted that she'd felt the same way about him as he did about her. Certainly, her actions had made him think that. A mistake which had left him broken-hearted and alone again. When she'd ended things so abruptly at Claire's house that day, he'd felt his whole world collapsing in on the future he'd imagined.

Not only was he staring death in the face again, but the woman he'd imagined being by his side for a long time had cut and run when he'd needed her most. A reminder not to rely on anyone. He could only count on himself, and had done since the day his father left.

However, it had come too late. It didn't matter how much he tried to deny it or wish it was otherwise. He was in love with Melissa. The only thing worse than being dumped at his sister's house and pretending he wasn't devastated in front of his family was not being able to speak to her.

Waiting to find out the results of his tests was going to be as torturous as not being with her, but he understood why she'd had to distance herself. She couldn't risk him not being around for the baby. It wasn't what he wanted either. Perhaps he should back off altogether and let her do the parenting without him in the picture.

After all, it might be something they would both have to get used to.

'Melissa!' Her patient's yell spurred Melissa upstairs with her bag in hand.

From the tone of Tess, her young mother, it was apparent something was wrong. That this wasn't the straightforward birth she'd expected. Nothing could have prepared Melissa for the sight awaiting her upstairs. A trail of blood led from the bathroom into the bedroom. She found the woman who wasn't due for another three weeks on the edge of the bed, her face pure white. A stark contrast to the scarlet stain spreading quickly over her trousers.

'Is this normal?' The terror in the young woman's voice and in her eyes almost broke Melissa. She was pleading with her to say everything was going to be all right, to do something, but Melissa couldn't make the promises she needed to hear.

Sometimes it was necessary to feel the fear and push ahead, hoping for the best outcome. The irony wasn't lost on her that she hadn't been able to do that in her own life.

'Lie on the bed and take deep breaths. I know it's difficult, but I need you to calm down. Deep breaths.' She simulated the action first, encouraging her to follow. The last thing they needed was for the patient's blood pressure to rise. Once she knew Tess was beginning to regulate her breathing, Melissa pulled her phone from her pocket.

'I'm calling an ambulance as a precaution because of the amount of blood you're losing. I'll just be out in the hall if you need me.' Melissa didn't want her to hear the anxiety in her voice as she relayed what was happening to the emergency services. If her patient was haemorrhaging, time was of the essence for mother and child.

'We'll try to get the ambulance to you within the hour,' the despatcher told her, as if this was an everyday occurrence and not a life-or-death situation.

'That's not good enough. I'm not sure we have an hour,' she hissed through gritted teeth, trying to keep her temper, but emphasising how serious the situation was.

'We'll get an ambulance to you as soon as we can.'

It was all Melissa could do not to throw the phone at the wall when she hung up, knowing she was on her own. Tess and the baby's lives were completely in her hands.

'Melissa, is my baby going to die?' Tess was sobbing when she rushed back into the bedroom. The patient was deathly pale and clearly terrified for her baby.

'Not if I can help it. Now I need to take a look and see what's happening.' She washed up and did an examination, checking in on baby too, whose heartbeat was slowing down. She had to move fast.

'Melissa?'

She knew Tess wanted her to say everything was all right, but she couldn't. If this was a placental abruption as she expected, the baby might not survive.

'We need to deliver the baby now. How far apart have the contractions been?'

'Just a couple of minutes.'

'Good.' At least baby was ready to be born, and that should make the delivery easier.

There was a risk of her bleeding out. Colour was draining out of her with every passing moment, and though Melissa had put in a cannula to replace lost fluids, she needed to be in the hospital.

Tess was likely going to need a blood transfusion, and it was lucky she was even still conscious.

'The ambulance is on the way. They'll get

you and baby transferred to the hospital, where we can look after you both better. In the meantime, we just need to get baby safely out. Next time a contraction hits, I want you to push, okay?' At least once the baby arrived, she could concentrate on the mother.

Tess nodded and grasped for her hand. 'Don't let go of me, okay?'

'I'm not going anywhere,' Melissa assured her.

'If anything happens to me, take care of the baby for me.' It was telling of this young woman's situation that she was asking a relative stranger to step in if the worst happened. Given Melissa's current circumstances, it was triggering for her.

Tess hadn't had a choice. The father of the baby abandoned her the moment she'd become pregnant. Melissa had purposely pushed Lachlan out of her life. That action would affect her baby's life, taking away the chance for them to bond with their father. She was capable of doing all of this on her own, but it was the reality of seeing this new mother struggling that made her realise she didn't have to. Deep down, she knew she didn't want to either.

'Nothing's going to happen. You just concentrate on seeing this little one come into the world.'

Tess's face contorted into a mask of pain as another contraction wracked her body.

'I'm going to need you to push, Tess.'

'I'm tired,' she wept.

'I know you are, sweetheart, but we have to get baby out. I'm going to need you to dig down deep. Your baby needs you to be strong for both of you.'

As her body contracted, Tess gritted her teeth and bore down with a scream.

'That's it. I can see baby's head. Focus on your breathing now for me.' Melissa could tell she was exhausted, her breaths interspersed with sobs, but they were nearly there.

Melissa coached her through the breathing techniques to stop her from pushing, leaving the baby to slither out on its own. She caught it quickly, wrapping it in a towel from the pile sitting at the end of the bed.

She cleaned the baby up, and the sound of it crying was the best thing she could have wished for.

'You have a little girl.' Melissa laid the child on her mother's chest.

Tess looked down at the baby with such undisguised love, Melissa was teary. Hoping she'd feel the same way about her baby too when the time came.

Tess gave a weak smile, barely able to open her eyes. 'A girl.'

'Stay awake for me. The ambulance will be here soon.' Although the bleeding was slowing, Tess needed a transfusion. She had to get to the hospital, and fast.

'Tess?' The new mother was beginning to lose consciousness. Melissa checked her pulse and found it was weakening.

This little girl needed her mother.

The weight off her chest when she heard the ambulance in the distance was short-lived. That pressure pushed down even stronger when she realised Tess was unconscious and had stopped breathing.

Melissa set the baby down in the crib at the side of the bed and started CPR on her mother. Arms out straight, fingers interlocked, she began pumping down on Tess's chest, counting out every compression. Then she stopped and looked for signs of life before continuing as long as her body would allow, her arms beginning to shake from the effort.

'One, two, three...' She kept going, stopping occasionally to listen to the heart, until eventually she was sure she detected a faint heartbeat.

Melissa put her ear to Tess's mouth and felt a little puff of air with the shallow breaths she was managing to take again.

She moved her into the recovery position and waited for help to arrive. Too tired to celebrate the rewards of her efforts, and too afraid in case it hadn't been enough after all.

'Hello?' a voice called from downstairs. Melissa ran out of the room to direct the paramedics upstairs as quickly as possible.

She relayed the seriousness of the situation as they rushed up the stairs, adding, 'She's lost a lot of blood.' As if they wouldn't see that for themselves.

Part of her wished Lachlan would be one of the crew in attendance to give her the sense of comfort and support she desperately needed. Disappointment settled in when he didn't appear.

The paramedics calmly set about preparing Tess for transporting, leaving Melissa to gather up the baby and hold her to her chest.

'Mummy's going to be all right,' she soothed, knowing she wouldn't be able to hold back the emotion much longer.

Especially when she thought of everything

that could go wrong in her own pregnancy. Having to go through it by herself like Tess, when Lachlan should be with her. She didn't want to even think of the possibility of leaving her baby on their own when the father wanted to be there for both of them.

If only she could move past the fear, she might still be able to keep him in her life. To have that family they both wanted.

Melissa wondered if she should get a pet to keep her company. Someone to talk to at the end of a difficult shift like last night's, even if it couldn't talk back. Despite living on her own for over a year and a half after Chris died, these weeks without Lachlan in her life had made her feel lonelier than ever. It had been nice to unwind with someone at the end of the day who understood the nature of her job, to swap stories with him, and simply have him to come home to. The house seemed bigger, emptier, without him filling her bed or making her cups of tea on demand. She missed him.

The nights were interminable at times. Never mind the physical side effects of the pregnancy keeping her awake—she also had thoughts of Lachlan swirling around her head.

About the past they'd shared, and the future they could have had if things had been different. If there wasn't the possibility of him getting sick. If she'd been braver...

She'd given up trying to have an early night, regardless of how weary she was. She sat up late watching trash TV into the early hours in the hope that she'd doze off and get some sort of sleep. Although tonight was proving particularly difficult with her back hurting, and she kept getting leg cramps. It was going to be fun when she really started to put on the extra weight and the baby started kicking her insides like a football. She definitely would have more sympathy with her pregnant ladies in future. All the textbooks and study hadn't taught her as much about what pregnancy entailed as having her own baby.

Lachlan sent her a text message every day just to make sure everything was okay, but it was difficult getting used to not having him in her life.

Lydia had been very good about checking in with her, but even if she was with her twenty-four hours a day, it wouldn't fill the void Lachlan had left in her life.

At least she had her work to focus on until the baby arrived.

'Congratulations again,' she told the couple sitting anxiously before her after confirming their pregnancy with positive test results.

Despite their want for a family, there wasn't even a hint of a smile in their reaction to the news, only more hand-holding and worried expressions.

'I'm afraid to get excited about it just yet,' Abby confessed. 'You know, after last time...'

The young woman had experienced an early miscarriage over a year ago and was understandably anxious, but there was nothing in her medical history to suggest the same thing would happen again. She didn't have any underlying conditions which would have contributed to her losing the baby. It was just one of those unfortunate things.

'I know you're worried, but there's absolutely no reason to think this won't be a viable pregnancy. Losing a baby is a painful, tragic thing, but you didn't do anything to cause that. Sometimes it just happens. Please don't let it spoil this pregnancy for you.'

'I'm just worried about what might happen. I'm afraid to look too far ahead in case we're devastated all over again.' Abby squeezed her husband's hand a little tighter, her grief for the baby she lost and fears for the one she was carrying evident.

'I promise we'll keep a close eye on you. Don't let what's happened in the past spoil your happiness. Enjoy every second.' The irony of her words wasn't lost on Melissa. She was equally guilty of letting her fears ruin what could have been the best thing to happen to her.

As the expectant couple thanked her for her reassurance and left with smiles on their faces, Melissa's thoughts were of her own loss. Of everything she'd thrown away with Lachlan because of her fears. She was equally guilty of letting the past destroy something good. Perhaps even worse than that, she was letting Lachlan go through potentially the most difficult time of his life alone.

Okay, so he had his family around, but the rejection he must've felt when she walked out of his life would've been crushing. Melissa winced, knowing all too well how that sense of abandonment impacted every area of life. She'd been so self-involved she hadn't considered how Lachlan would cope with everything on his own. The same sort of behaviour she'd held against her parents for years. If she couldn't forgive them, how could she expect Lachlan to forgive her?

And she realised, likely too late, that that was what she wanted. Forgiveness. Lachlan. A family.

She was in love with him, and that's what she'd been running from, afraid to face it in case she lost him. However, the prospect of not having him in her life at all seemed worse than making the most of whatever time they could have together. They could be a family, even for a short while, and she hoped it wasn't too late to try.

She loved him and wanted to be there for him, if only he'd still let her.

Lachlan came out of the consultant's office stunned by the news of his latest results. He was in a kind of limbo, not knowing where to go from here now that he didn't have Melissa to turn to.

They should've been planning for the baby's arrival. Any other father-to-be would be painting a nursery and building furniture, but he'd been left on the outside, not sure if he would even have a part in his child's life.

He didn't know whether it would've changed things if he'd told her he loved her. Probably not, when it had been too much even for him to deal with. This time apart hadn't eased the situation for him. It had only served to prove the depth of his feelings for her. His sense of loss was very real. Not only because Melissa was no longer in his life, but his whole future, the family he'd realised he wanted after all, was gone with her.

He might never have another chance to have a child. Not that he would want one with anyone else anyway. She'd been the only person who'd managed to make him take that risk. Now he was grieving for the loss of it all.

So much so, he even imagined he could see her now walking towards him. Probably because all he wanted was a hug from her and a promise that everything was going to be okay. Too much to ask for, given the circumstances, but since it was his hallucination, he figured he could wish for the world.

Then suddenly she flung her arms around him, and he swore he could feel her warmth, smell her sweet perfume, and hear her voice in his ear.

'Claire told me you'd be here. I'm so sorry, Lachlan.' Melissa squeezed him hard enough he had to believe she was real, if only to tell her to let go.

'I can't…breathe,' he said, though he'd never been so happy to almost suffocate.

'Sorry.' She let go and took a step back.

'You're really here.' He couldn't believe his eyes, but his slightly bruised ribs would testify to the fact she wasn't a figment of his imagination after all.

'I am. I hope that's okay. I know I'm probably the last person you want to see right now.'

That simply wasn't true. She was the only person he'd wanted to see, but he didn't want to get too carried away when she'd made it clear the last time he'd seen her that she no longer wanted to be part of his life.

'Why are you here?' He moved out of the main corridor to a quieter area so they could talk in private.

'I'm sorry for how I left things. I've had time to think everything over, and I know I reacted badly. I should have been there to support you. Is it too late to do that now?'

Lachlan didn't know what had prompted this sudden act of conscience, and though he was grateful to see her, he didn't want her to be here simply out of guilt. It occurred to him that because of Claire, she was aware he was here to discuss the results of his cancer tests. He didn't want the outcome of those to influence her reasons for coming to see him.

'What do you want, Melissa? You made it clear that you no longer wanted to be involved with me on a personal level. What's changed?' He'd already been let down by her once, and he needed to know he'd be able to count on her in the future if the worst did happen. More than that, he needed to know she felt the same way about him as he did about her, or else he was always going to be the one to get hurt.

She hung her head, looking thoroughly ashamed. 'I panicked. When you said the cancer might be back, I thought of the impact that losing you would have on me and stupidly believed that if I backed away now, it would somehow lessen the pain. It was selfish of me to think that way.'

'So how do you feel now?' His heart was beating fast as he fought to control the hope that there could still be a chance for them. As much as he still wanted to be with her, he had to be sure of her motives and commitment. It wouldn't be fair on him or the baby if she decided again somewhere down the line that she didn't want him to be involved in their lives. As he'd said from the start, he wanted to be a proper father, and he had to value that over his own wants. If Melissa was only here because she felt sorry for him, they weren't going to be able to sustain anything long-term.

Melissa swallowed hard. 'I love you, Lachlan. That's why I was so afraid of losing you. But these past days without you have shown me that I still want you in my life for as long as I have you. I'll support you through your treatment, and we'll both be there for our baby as long as we can. That's all we can do, and more than I probably deserve.'

It meant a lot for him to hear her say that now, when the future seemed so uncertain and terrifying. She loved him. She wanted to be with him. And he knew how much that cost her to admit. Melissa was opening her heart to him, leaving herself vulnerable when there was a chance he could reject her. After everything she'd gone through with her parents and Chris, he knew this couldn't have been easy for her, and she wouldn't have said these things unless she meant them. Now it was down to him to be equally as brave. Even if it meant risking his heart again too.

'You deserve happiness, Melissa. Come to think of it, so do I.' He reached out and pulled her back into his arms, hugging her close to his chest, never wanting to let her go. There was no point in letting pride, fear, or ill health steal away what joy they had.

Melissa bunched his shirt in her fist. 'I just want us to be together. I'm sorry I was too scared to tell you that in the first place. But I'll be by your side for as long as you want me.'

'Hopefully, that's going to be for a long time to come.'

Melissa pried herself away from his chest to look up at him. For once he had some good news to share. He hoped it wouldn't change things between them except for the better.

'My test results were clear. It was a lot of worry over nothing. The cancer hasn't come back after all.'

He saw the tears welling in Melissa's eyes right before she buried her head in his chest again.

'I'm so happy for you, Lachlan.'

'That's not to say it won't ever return, but we'll cross that bridge if we come to it.'

'Together.'

That one word cemented their future. A promise and a commitment to each other and their baby. There would be no more looking back, only forward. To their life as a family.

Yes, he'd been guilty of holding back, of

bottling his feelings. But losing her had made him see just how damned important she was to him. Melissa had never just been a casual lover, or someone he'd got pregnant by accident. She was the woman he loved. Someone he wanted to spend the rest of his life with. However long that would be. He would take a few years with her over a lifetime without her. If she'd have him.

Lachlan had spent his whole life doing the right thing, mindful of other people's feelings, and it was time to go for what he wanted. That was Melissa. The baby. A family.

Melissa reached out a hand and stroked Lachlan's cheek. 'I love you, Lachlan. You're here, now. That's all that matters. I can guarantee our baby would rather have you around for as long as possible than not at all. As would I. Besides, you're young, strong and incredibly handsome, and I will challenge cancer to a fight over you every day of the week. Please stay. Please love me.'

She sounded desperate, but if there was any chance they could be together, she was grabbing it and not letting go. If he loved her and wanted to be with her, then she was going to make sure they made this work. She wasn't losing anyone else she loved.

'I love you, Melissa. I think I always have, and I know I always will. We might have skipped straight from meeting into starting a family, but I'd like the chance to have that whole bit in between too. I want to be with you.'

'Honestly?'

'I honestly, truly, want to be with you. It's all I want.' He leaned down and sealed his admission of love for her with a kiss.

Melissa would be an idiot to say no now when he was giving her everything she ever wanted.

EPILOGUE

'WELL, MY PARENTS love you,' Melissa said as she manoeuvred herself into bed. At eight months pregnant, it wasn't becoming any easier. Nor was sleeping when she couldn't get comfortable at all. She was looking forward to having control over her body again almost as much as meeting their baby.

'Naturally. Old Jilly, Angus, and I get on like a house on fire. That's why they wanted to meet me so badly,' Lachlan teased, climbing in beside her.

He'd encouraged her to reach out to her parents and try to reconnect. After some soul-searching, she'd come to the conclusion that they deserved a second chance too, and thankfully they'd been overjoyed to hear from her. Apparently, they hadn't wanted to interfere in her life since they'd parted on bad terms, but loved her nonetheless. For the past few months, they'd been speaking a lot, clearing the air, and chatting over video calls. That was how they'd got to know Lachlan. She was pretty sure they'd come over as much to meet him as the baby. They were staying in the UK for the next couple of months until she gave birth, and hopefully beyond. There was even talk of moving back so they could see their grandchild, and Melissa, on a regular basis.

'You're so modest.' She cuddled into him as close as her huge bump would allow. There was nothing better at the end of the day than to be in his arms, feeling his love for her. In a few weeks' time, there would be an addition to their nightly routine, and she thought her heart would burst at the happiness coming into her life.

When Chris had died, she'd thought the idea of having a family was over forever. Thanks to Lachlan, not only was she going to have one of her own, but she had her parents here to be part of it. His recent oncology check-up had also been positive, giving him the all-clear. Everything was looking bright for the future.

'Hey, if I'd been shy, we might never have got together.'

Melissa nudged him with an elbow. 'Um…

I think you'll find I was the one who walked over to you first.'

'Only because I'd been staring at you, and it was obvious I was interested. You knew it was safe to approach.'

'Well, I'm happy I did.' She tilted her face up to kiss him, glad she'd had the courage to finally move on from Chris, or else she'd still be on her own.

'Best day of my life was meeting you.' Lachlan dipped his head and kissed her again. 'Marry me?'

'What?' Melissa wrenched her mouth away from his, unsure she was hearing him right.

He twisted his body around so she could see his face. 'I mean it. Marry me. There's still time before the baby comes to make it official. We can be a proper family.'

Melissa eyed him with some suspicion. Though he showed her and told her he loved her every day, she still needed reassurance that he wanted to do this for the right reasons. Because there was nothing she wanted more than to spend the rest of her life with this man.

'And before you start questioning my motives, I'm asking because I love you. I don't want to waste another moment without you.

I want nothing more than to make our family complete, and I'll spend my life proving to you how much I love you. Melissa Moran, will you marry me?'

'Yes, Lachlan McNairn. I would love to be your wife.'

Melissa looked into the eyes of the man she loved, the father of her unborn baby, and knew without doubt he was committed to her, body and soul. She was no longer alone.

* * * * *

If you enjoyed this story, check out these other great reads from Karin Baine

An American Doctor in Ireland
A Mother for His Little Princess
Surgeon Prince's Fake Fiancée
Nurse's Risk with the Rebel

All available now!